Treasure Isla

By

Lynda L. Lock

&

your FRIEND Sparky

Dedication – Paradise Lost

Lawrie Lock: March 3rd 1942 – September 3rd 2018

Paradise is usually a place, but for me, paradise is a person; my husband, adventure partner, world-traveler, lover, dance partner, and best friend—Lawrie Lock.

He was always my rock, my inspiration, and my sounding board. We've traveled the world together, getting into mischief, sticky situations, and occasionally heated arguments that revolved around a finicky classic car doing something weird.

His diagnosis of Rapid Onset ALS caught us by surprise, and the speed with which Lawrie declined into complete paralysis took our breath away. But through it all, he smiled that killer-gorgeous smile and tried to make the best of a horrific situation. He slipped away on September 3rd, 2018, at home, looking at the beautiful Caribbean Sea.

If the rain is liquid sunshine, then my tears are liquid love. I will love you to my last breath.

Intro

My first novel, Treasure Isla, was hatched in a laughter-filled conversation with my husband, Lawrie. Waiting for the full moon to rise out of the Caribbean Sea, we were settled with a glass of wine on the upper deck of our home on Isla Mujeres.

"I going to write a mystery novel about Isla Mujeres and the pirates that visited here," I said.

"Great idea," he replied.

Then I noticed that our wine glasses were empty. "I'll be right back," I said, grabbing both glasses and heading downstairs to the kitchen.

Five minutes later I returned and handed the refilled glass to him.

"I've got an idea for the name of the first book and the plot," he said and proceeded to rattle off the storyline of a twenty-something Canadian woman and her Mexicana friend who lived, worked, and partied with the other young singles. In his storyline, the two women had heard rumors about Captain Fermin Mundaca's buried treasure and decided to search for it.

I burst into laughter. "I was only gone five minutes!"

He smiled and tapped his head with one finger. "You know me. Always cooking up ideas."

And Treasure Isla was born. The characters are a compilation of several of my island friends; Mexicans and foreigners. They are adventurous, carefree people who work hard, party hard, and live completely in the moment.

Life on a tropical island is an adventure.

Life on a tropical island when you are young at heart is a blast!

Prologue

May 1683

Screams of anguish washed over the pirate encampment on the Island of Sacrifices, *la Isla de Sacrificios,* as a dozen hostages were slaughtered. Their severed heads were carelessly tossed into a nearby launch, sightless eyes turned beseechingly towards the heavens, begging to be saved. As an inducement for the surviving residents, the gruesome cargo was ferried from the island and flung ashore in the Port of Veracruz. *Pay up. Pay now, or the remainder of the captives will meet the same fate.*

"Bastard!" roared a tall blond man. "Van Hoorn, you animal, fight me now. The winner takes all."

The clamor of metal pulverizing metal exploded through the humid air, causing the tense watchers to wince in pain. Sparks erupted with the ferocity of the blows. Thrusting back against their crossed swords, the combatants regrouped. Hunting for a killing strike, the lean muscular men warily circled each other like powerful lions stalking their prey. Captain Laurens Cornelis Boudewijn de Graaf, nicknamed the *Scourge of the West,* fought Captain Nikolaas Van Hoorn for the fate of their captives.

On May 13th, thirteen ships and nearly fifteen hundred battle-hardened men invaded Veracruz, the Spanish colonial city on the eastern side of Mexico, killing over four hundred citizens before finally subduing the population. The invaders had ransacked and burned their way through the town before fleeing with their hostages to the eerie Island of Sacrifices, *la Isla de Sacrificios*. Here, amongst the ancient ghosts of the indigenous people sacrificed to an almost forgotten god, the pirates anxiously waited. The ransom payment for the remaining captives was taking too long for the liking of Van Hoorn. He was impatient to set sail before the Spanish mounted a retaliatory attack. It was he who ordered the beheadings.

The two captains lunged, parried, collided, slashed, and regrouped repeatedly. Neither gave quarter to the other until a swift strike by de Graaf sliced Van Hoorn's sword-fighting arm to the bone.

Van Hoorn stumbled; his weapon dropped from his battered hand. "Yield," he shouted, agony echoing in his voice. His good hand clamped painfully over the damaged wrist, attempting to curb the blood flow.

Panting with exertion, de Graaf touched the tip of his weapon into the notch of his opponent's throat as he said, "The hostages are mine now."

Van Hoorn silently nodded in agreement, his eyes burning with humiliation and rage.

"Leave." His jaw muscles bunched with tension, de Graaf pulled his sword back, pointing towards the anchored fleet. "Leave before I change my mind."

Van Hoorn supported his damaged arm with his good one, motioning with his chin that he wanted a subordinate to retrieve his favorite sword.

De Graaf derisively wagged the tip of his blade, "No, that's mine too."

De Graaf stood comfortably spread-legged on the deck of his ship. He had recently captured the 40-gun treasure ship, the *San Francisco,* from the Spanish Armada and renamed it the *Francesa*.

The big ship slid over the turquoise water, inching towards the narrow end of the lagoon. Shrouded by palm trees and low-growing dense thickets of mangroves, the inlet was shallow in places but calm and safe. It had been a few weeks since the siege at Veracruz and his sword fight with Van Hoorn. Rumor amongst his compatriots was that his opponent had died two weeks later from gangrene originating from his wounded wrist. Ah, well. It could just as easily have been him instead of Van Hoorn.

De Graaf's blond mane curled where it touched his shoulders. One hand rested casually on the handle of his cutlass where the scabbard was attached to his leather belt, the other on his dagger. Long leggings were tucked into tall black boots. His embroidered white shirt was unlaced at the throat, allowing the slight breeze to dry his sweating chest.

"Isla Mujeres." He smiled wolfishly as he rolled the Spanish name over his tongue. "Maybe we'll find some pretty women on this island."

Chapter 1

Día de los Muertos

"What a stupid idea," said the thin blond as she staggered down the narrow stone-paved street, a bottle of Don Julio tequila swaying precariously in her right hand. Her left arm, decorated with an intricate tattoo of dolphins, colorful sea turtles, and a whale shark, was tightly wrapped around her friend's shoulders.

Yasmin Medina hiccupped, "Jessica, be quiet."

"Digging up a dead pirate on the Día de los Muertos, the Day of the Dead," Jessica Sanderson flung her head back and laughed.

"Shut up. We don't want to get caught. This is a very important night on the island and in all of Mexico. Families usually spend the evening with their dead loved ones, sharing favorite food and drinks." Yasmin grabbed the bottle of tequila and slurped back another mouthful. "My grandmother says the pirate Fermin Mundaca isn't really buried in this grave. But the legend is that he left a clue to where he buried his treasure, and it could be here." She stumbled on the uneven pavers, "Damn stilettos. They have to go." Yasmin roughly pulled the red, thin-heeled shoes from her feet, gripping the delicate leather straps with one hand and clutching her friend with the other. They continued towards the cemetery in Centro.

"So, tell me, why hasn't anyone else in the last two hundred years come up with this freaking brilliant idea of digging up Mundaca to find the clue?"

"Fear? Suspicion? Belief in evil spirits?" Yasmin said, shrugging. "Who knows?"

Grinning at her friend, Jessica Sanderson giggled between hiccups, "Dark curly hair, brown skin, and green eyes, you could be a descendent of La Trigueña, that beautiful teenage Mexican chick that the old disease-ridden fool was so horny for."

"My grandmother says I do look like her. The blond streaks in my dark hair are the same as La Trigueña's. Her nickname means brunette." Yasmin thought for a moment then continued, "It's disgusting when you think about it. A fifty-something-year-old man who wants to marry a sixteen-year-old. He was old enough to be her grandfather."

"Why exactly are we here on such a busy night?" Jessica's eyebrows quirked up, questioning their less-than-reasoned decision.

"I told you, the graveyard is normally locked after sundown, but it's left open for family members to visit on this special night. Four in the morning is perfect. It's the quiet time." The often-painted iron gates of the centuries-old cemetery were propped open, giving all-night access for families celebrating the *Día de los Muertos*. "The trick is to look like we belong here," Yasmin said as they walked through the gates.

The two young women drunkenly meandered between the tightly packed monuments decorated with deep yellow marigolds, personal trinkets, special treats, and drinks to share with the dead. Watchful stone angels seemed to glare at the inebriated intruders. "This is spooky," Jessica whispered.

"There, that's it." Yasmin pointed at a unique, low-to-the-ground stone crypt, far too short for a body. Mundaca had commissioned the construction of this tomb in 1879, before his death. His actual grave is in Mérida, a larger city in the Yucatan peninsula, where he died. Crowded by more recent additions to the graveyard, the top of the vault was about knee-high to Yasmin and decorated with what appeared to be chess figures: a bishop perhaps in the center of the lid and four pawns guarding the corners. One of the pawn-shaped figures had been irregularly snapped off, likely the victim of vandalism. Yasmin studied the monument, trying to figure out how to open the chamber. "Damn it. We should have brought some tools."

Jessica had noticed a caretaker's shack off to the left when they entered the cemetery, "Wait a minute, let me see what I can find." Beginning to sober up, she nonchalantly sauntered towards the small building. Standing on tippy toes, she pressed her face close to the window near the door. She saw a couple of shovels, some machetes, and a long metal bar. *Perfect.* With a quick glance around, she tried the doorknob, but it was locked. Then she pulled off her shoe and bashed a hole in the window with her stiletto heel, quickly brushing aside the broken glass and reaching inside to unlatch the door.

Jessica got her resourceful attitude from her two older brothers, Jake and Matt. They were punks as teenagers, pulling borderline illegal pranks just for laughs. In recent years they had confided to Jessica over several tongue-loosening beers just how badly behaved they had been. Now they were both respected citizens in their hometown and dedicated firefighters.

Lugging a shovel and the heavy iron bar back to where Yasmin was still puzzling over how to open the grave, Jessica dropped the tools with a clank.

Startled, Yasmin's head popped up, "Shhh. You're too noisy."

"Sorry. They're heavy." Jessica stood barefoot like her friend on the warm sandy earth, examining the stone crypt. "So there has to be a crack somewhere that I can slide this bar into and pry something loose," she mumbled, running a finger along the seams of the stone blocks. "Yep. Right here." Jessica inserted the pry bar and heaved with all her strength. Nothing. "Damn it." She tried again, standing on the bar in her bare feet, bouncing lightly. Nothing. "Yasmin, get over here. I need help."

Between the combined efforts of the two slim women bouncing up and down on the metal pry bar, an end piece shifted slightly. They hopped down, repositioned, and tried again. A bit more of a shift. Again and again, they tried until finally, the space was large enough for Yasmin to slip her slender hand into the crevice.

"Really, you're just going to stick your hand in there? You're not worried about spiders and scorpions?" Jessica's Nordic-blue eyes flicked a glance at her friend. *Just how much tequila had she drunk?*

"Well, what do you expect me to do? We don't have a flashlight, and neither one of us smokes, so we don't have a lighter. Should I just step into the street and holler, 'hey, anyone got a light?'" Yasmin knelt and reached inside, carefully feeling around the empty space, hoping like hell that no nasty critters lurked inside. *Nothing.* But there, with the tip of her fingers, she could feel something smooth and metal. She slowly drew the object towards her and pulled it free from the crypt.

"What the hell? A flask," muttered Jessica, "a stupid whisky flask, so he didn't get thirsty on his final journey. Damn it."

Yasmin stared dejectedly at the dull metal item. "All that effort for this." The top was stuck tight with age and dirt. She shook the container, but nothing. No noise, no sloshing sounds, no rattle of gold. Zero.

Jessica picked up the metal bar. "Come on, girl. We need to replace this chunk of stone and get out of here. The two women struggled and heaved, gradually easing the end piece into its original position. Jessica tilted her head, noticing the new scrape marks on the stone. She quickly smoothed dirt over the raw white scratches. Tired, barefoot, and bedraggled, they replaced the tools in the caretaker's shack and trudged out the cemetery gates.

As dawn broke over the Caribbean Sea on the eastern side of Isla Mujeres, the Island of Women, the two weary women hailed a taxi and headed home for a few hours of sleep before work. Yasmin snoozed in the cab's backseat, clutching the dull metal flask in her left hand.

Chapter 2

November 3rd Morning

"Oh, God, I was overserved last night." Yasmin Medina moaned, pulling the covers back and gingerly stepping on the cool tile floor. "*La cruda*, a hangover — too much tequila." Glancing at the time on her smartphone, she yelped as she realized she had overslept. "Oh, shit. I can't be late again, or Carlos will fire me."

She scrambled to find fresh underwear, clean shorts, and her work t-shirt and dashed into the shower. Not waiting for the water to warm up, she danced around under the weak stream of cold water, trying her best to freshen up without chilling her sensitive areas.

Dressed and with a bit of eye makeup slapped on, Yasmin dashed out the door and waved frantically at a passing taxi, "Come on. Please stop. You've got room for one skinny woman," she muttered. "Yes." The taxi stopped, and Yasmin squished into the back seat with two larger women.

"Buenos Dias, Centro, the *Loco Lobo* por favor," she told the driver.

As the passengers silently rode toward the center of town, Yasmin thumbed through her messages. There were several from Jessica, becoming more frantic as time passed. *Hey, are you awake yet? Call me.* And later: *Yasmin, call me. It's getting late. You have to be at work soon.* And still later: *Hey girl, wake up. Get your butt into work — now.*

Rapidly thumbing a reply, *I'm coming. I'm on the way.* Yasmin leaned back in the seat, idly scanning the neighborhood streets as the taxi wove and darted through the thick afternoon traffic.

Thousands of tourists, day-trippers from the Cancun hotel zone, came to Isla Mujeres for the novel experience of driving a golf cart around the seven-kilometer island. The tourists were a blessing and a curse. The blessing: tourists were the reason the restaurants, beach clubs, and bars employed thousands of islanders. The curse: they clogged the streets with rental golf carts and typically drove like self-absorbed teenagers. In the narrow streets of Centro, built before vehicles had been invented, there was very little space. All the downtown roads, except two, were one-way-only narrow avenues stuffed with parked cars, careening golf carts, and large delivery trucks. The lack of clear signage created havoc. Visitors had no idea which streets ran north or which were for southbound traffic only. The east-west designations were not clear either, causing near-misses, and repeated shouts of "Wrong way!" as the oblivious drivers powered toward oncoming traffic. Relief from the mayhem usually arrived at sundown when the tour boats returned to the much larger city of Cancun and its late-night activities.

Yasmin and her workmate, Jessica Sanderson, lived near each other but separately, renting reasonably affordable tiny houses, *casitas,* located in the *colonias.* Her neighborhood in the *colonias* was where tiny store-front businesses intermingled with equally cramped living spaces. The dentist's office was tucked behind the air conditioning and appliance repair shop, and the aluminum fabricator sat beside a two-washing-machine laundromat. Yasmin loved living in the noisy, crowded, and boisterous area. Her neighbors knew her and her entire family. It was home.

Her diminutive *casita* shared common walls with the homes on both sides. The dwelling contained one bedroom, a bathroom, a minuscule kitchen, and a living area complete with hooks for additional hammocks firmly anchored in the walls. Jessica was luckier. Her house was a little larger, with a tiny second bedroom and a small fenced backyard, just large enough for a bistro-style table and two chairs. It was the perfect location to catch a cooling breeze in the evening.

Smiling to herself, Yasmin had to admit that even though they were good friends, she couldn't share a house with Jessica. The two of them were so very different. Jessica was an exuberant early riser. No matter how late they partied the night before, she was up early singing off-key as she ricocheted around her kitchen while making coffee. Jessica had recently admitted that her guilt complex woke her up at dawn. The early bird gets the worm and all that other stuff that her Canadian grandparents had instilled in her childhood brain. On the other hand, in Yasmin's own Mexican culture, late-night partying was frequently followed by civilized late-morning sleeping, and that was a sore point with their boss Carlos Mendoza. He enjoyed the relaxed Mexican lifestyle, but he was also a businessman and expected his staff to show up on time for their shifts.

Running awkwardly in her high heels from the corner where the taxi driver dropped her off, Yasmin scooted into the bar seconds before she spotted her boss. She nonchalantly picked up a cloth to wipe the sticky granite countertop, shouting a cheery "Hola" to Carlos and pretending she had been there all along.

"Since you are obviously working so hard, perhaps you should put your shoulder bag in the staff area," he greeted her with a sardonic grin. "No need to wear it while you work." His handsome features were slightly flawed by a scar that ran from his left eyebrow to the corner of his mouth, a fading souvenir of a misspent youth. A head taller than Yasmin, Carlos was dressed in pressed tan chinos and a long-sleeved black linen shirt with the cuffs folded back to expose well-muscled forearms. The contrast between his coffee-colored skin and perfectly white teeth could make her sweat if her thoughts lingered too long. His leather sandals were tropical casual and looked expensive. No gold chains, no rings, just his Rolex watch on his left wrist.

Carlos casually sauntered towards the back of the building, sighing as he shut the door to his office, "Yasmin, Yasmin. It's a good thing you are so very beautiful." His buddy Diego had said he was so overwhelmed by her smile that he forgot to check to see if she had boobs. Well, yes, she had boobs, and great long legs, and a tight little butt. She was just freaking beautiful—and nice. So, he cut her a lot of slack when he should fire that sweet little ass.

She was his most senior employee, coming up to three years next month, and she was an outstanding bartender. Still, some of the other employees were jealous of what they viewed as preferential treatment, but if he did fire Yasmin for not being punctual, his regular male customers would be highly annoyed. It was a no-win situation. Besides, if he was honest with himself, he liked her— a lot. A whole hell of a lot. So, he pretended to be upset with her for appearance's sake, but in reality, it would take a lot more than just being occasionally late for him to fire her.

Fool, he thought. He worked seven days a week at the bar because he didn't know what else to do with his time. He was childless, recently divorced, and paying alimony to his ex-wife. And now he was mooning like a love-sick teenager over a younger woman who probably thought a thirty-nine-year-old man was old enough to be her father. "Get a grip, man."

Behind the bar counter, Jessica quickly pressed the camera app on her phone, laughing at the expression on Yasmin's face, and snapped a photo. "Oh, my gawd. You're so busted! The look on your face is priceless." She keyed into her Instagram account and sent the image to Yasmin's phone.

Yasmin stuttered, not sure what to say, then she laughed.

"By the way, what about the thing we 'found' last night?" Jessica asked, sliding her phone into her back pocket. "What did you do with it?"

Yasmin was momentarily perplexed by Jessica's question. "What thing?"

"That metal flask," Jessica whispered, "you know, from the graveyard."

"Oh, right. I brought it with me," Yasmin rummaged in her oversized shoulder bag, "I haven't had time to look at it because I slept in." She quickly looked around and pulled the flask out. "It's a bit ordinary looking for a rich pirate to own, don't you think?" She held it down behind the bar, visible enough for Jessica to see.

The flask was a dull metal with a bit of engraving and an old piece of cork stoppering the mouth. Jessica reached over and tugged on the cork, popping it out. "Hey," she whispered, "there's something inside. Let's see what it is."

Tipping the container over, Yasmin gently tapped it on the palm of her hand, slowly dislodging the article. A ragged end of rolled paper poked out of the neck of the bottle. She inserted her pinky finger into the center of the roll and twisted it tighter so that the whole piece of paper could slide out into her hand. She ran a hand over the smooth granite surface of the bar, checking for moisture before carefully setting the paper down. Yasmin gently held the curled edges with both hands so that she could see the writing. "Holy cow," she murmured, "it's a letter written by Fermin Mundaca to La Trigueña."

"Seriously?" Jessica grabbed her cell phone, "Wait. Wait. Let me get a photo." She snapped a picture, then made a rolling motion with her hand. "Turn it over so I can get the other side." She clicked her camera app, then lightly tapped the page. "Is that a map?"

"Careful. The paper is fragile." Yasmin peered at the squiggles on the paper. "Maybe it's a map. I'm not sure."

"Can you read the letter?"

Turning the page back over, Yasmin studied the flowing script. "The ink is quite faded, and the words are an ancient and formal style of Spanish, but I can get most of it."

"I think it says, *"My dearest sweetheart, I am leaving you everything I have in the world because I love you. When I built the hacienda that I intended to share with you, I uncovered the treasure buried by Captain Lorencillo de Graaf. I have been told de Graaf was the Dutchman who, in 1683, raided the rich Spanish stronghold of Veracruz. I have moved the valuables to a safer place, and this letter will help you find the location. This is what I give to you. I will love you forever, Fermin Mundaca."*

Holding the letter in her shaking hands, Yasmin looked at Jessica, "Are you kidding me?" she whispered. "Buried treasure."

"Yes!" Jessica exclaimed, pumping her fist into the air. "We're gonna be rich, freaking rich."

"Shhh. Shhh, be quiet." Yasmin quickly checked for anyone who might be listening to their conversation. "First of all, he says he moved it, so we have to locate it, and secondly, I'm not sure about the legality of us claiming the treasure. We did, after all, steal this from his empty crypt."

"Borrowed, we just borrowed it." Jessica deadpanned.

"Jessica, what do you mean, borrowed? We broke into his grave and took the flask and this letter. That's stealing."

"Nope. We intend to return it, so it is just borrowed." Jessica had a mischievous smirk on her lips. "That's what my granddad called it."

"Are you serious?" Yasmin sputtered.

Jessica held up a placating hand, "You have to understand the circumstances. My grandparents on my dad's side lived in a remote gold mining town in the mountains of British Columbia. There were several abandoned mining communities scattered in the area. People in the occupied towns normally took things left behind in the deserted towns — things like pots, pans, dishes, hand tools, or bed frames. It was just stuff that was too costly to move when the mine closed, and the workers had to relocate to another community. Call it repurposing or recycling if that makes you feel better." Jessica grinned at Yasmin's surprised expression, adding, "We are just borrowing this map. We can always return it after we find the treasure."

Chapter 3

November 3rd Evening

"Okay, just one drink tonight. I need to sleep," Yasmin covered her yawn with a hand. "I am so damn tired."

"Yeah, yeah, whatever." Jessica good-naturedly flapped a hand, dismissing Yasmin's complaint.

When their four-to-midnight shift finished, Yasmin and Jessica wandered down the street to their favorite place to relax. Open until two in the morning, *El Arrecife, The Reef,* was the gathering place for other restaurant workers unwinding after work.

They turned at the sign with a painted arrow indicating the doorway hidden behind the spreading branches of a large almond tree. The entrance and stairway walls were painted cerulean blue, depicting an ocean brimming with colorful fish and sea creatures. Yasmin climbed the stairway to the second floor, crossing to her favorite spot—a row of stools set along the open side of the bar with a view of the street scene below.

"Let's look at that letter again." Jessica signaled the bartender for two of their regular drinks, frozen ginger margaritas, no salt. The combination of the sharp bite of freshly crushed ginger, the tang of the tequila, and the acidic lime really perked up the brain cells. In her mind, it was a healthier alternative to a shot of Red Bull, the high-energy, high-caffeine drink so popular amongst her friends.

Carefully removing the delicate piece of paper from her purse, Yasmin said, "we have to get this copied and put the original someplace safe. This paper is too brittle for us to keep handling it." Yasmin examined the ornate handwriting, "It doesn't say much more than what I read earlier." Turning the letter over in her hands, Yasmin pointed at the black, irregular squiggles on the back of the paper. "I wonder what this means?" She tilted her head to the right, puzzling over the wavy lines. "If I turn the page the other way up, there's a compass drawn on the top right corner. Maybe the lines indicate the shoreline? Can't be a mountain because there aren't any on Isla."

Jessica poked her head closer to Yasmin's hands. "It must be a map. Mundaca said the letter would help *La Trigueña* find the treasure. It has to be a clue, but it's pretty darn vague." Frustrated by the lack of information, Jessica reached for her quickly disappearing margarita. "By the way, who the hell is Captain Lorencillo de Graaf? I thought we were looking for Mundaca's treasure."

"Well, that's another story my grandmother told me. De Graaf was a very successful pirate who, along with three other famous buccaneers, Nikolaas Van Hoorn, Michel de Grammont, and Pierre Bot, attacked the town of Veracruz in 1683, I think. Between the five of them, they commanded a fleet of a dozen ships and more than a thousand fighting men."

Deep in thought, her eyes veered off to the side as she recalled more of the story. She absentmindedly sipped her drink and continued, "Sailing two captured Spanish galleons at the head of the fleet, the invaders tricked the townspeople into thinking it was the scheduled arrival of the Spanish Armada. The pirates stormed the fortified town, killing soldiers and residents. One, Captain Van Hoorn, landed his troops further up the coast, and his horde attacked from the land side of the city. Most of the townspeople were barricaded inside a church while the pirates threatened to burn it to the ground. It must have been awful. More than four hundred people died during the attack."

27

Yasmin slurped her margarita, tipping the glass up to catch the last remaining drops. "The governor was hiding in the city, and the pirates ransomed him back to Spain for seventy thousand pieces of eight. That's part of the treasure supposedly hidden on Isla by de Graaf."

Jessica waved two fingers at the bartender again, "Dos más por favor." One, two, what did it matter? There was lots of time to sleep it off. "Wow, what a great story. But how much are seventy thousand pieces of...whatever, worth now?"

"Well, it's worth a whole lot more than we currently have in our bank accounts, that's for sure. And Isla was a favorite hiding place for many different pirates. It was relatively uninhabited, with no soldiers, or government officials, just a few fishermen and their families. The sheltered west side, near Makax Lagoon, was perfect for beaching and repairing their boats. Fresh fish and turtle meat were a good source of protein, plus coconuts for vitamins. Turquoise water, white sandy beaches. It would have been a perfect haven."

"So, these squiggly lines? Maybe the cove where de Graaf landed his ship?" Yasmin was concentrating on the piece of paper and didn't notice as Jessica slipped a fresh drink close to her hand.

"Well, hi there, gorgeous." A tall, fit man with dark hair wrapped an arm around Yasmin. The top of her head grazed his chin as he pulled her closer. She could feel the well-developed muscles in his arms and chest. Annoyed at his casual intimacy, Yasmin shrugged his arm away, moving over onto the next stool to reclaim her personal space. She hugged her arms tightly around her body as she watched the shorter guy, with blond hair and green eyes, sidle up to Jessica.

"I'm Ryan Whitecross from Minneapolis," the blond said as he cocked a thumb towards his friend, "and he's Kirk Patterson from Key West."

"Hi, I've seen you both at the *Loco Lobo*," Jessica responded lightly. "How're you guys doing tonight?"

Ryan snapped his fingers, "That's right. You're a server, and your friend here is a bartender."

Jessica nodded. "Yeah, that's us."

Glancing at the paper in Yasmin's hands, Whitecross said. "Hey, what's that? It looks really old." He reached to take the paper from her hands, but she quickly slid it inside her large purse.

"Just a note from my grandmother asking me to come and visit her next weekend." She glanced at Jessica, silently telling her not to say anything about their find. She finally noticed the fresh drink beside her; *oh well, one more won't hurt, I guess.*

Pointing at himself and at Kirk, Ryan motioned to the bartender for two beers.

An hour later, after drinking part of a third margarita, Yasmin was feeling light-headed from alcohol and lack of sleep. "Hey girl, I'm done. You want to share a taxi?"

"Nope. I'm good. I'll find my way home later."

To Yasmin's eyes, Jessica's expression resembled a cat anticipating a tasty meal. "Okay, be careful. See you later." Tomorrow was their day off, a day to sleep late, do laundry, and restock the fridge.

As she started down the stairway, she turned and glanced over her left shoulder. The guy named Kirk was staring at her; his unsmiling blue eyes raked upwards before settling on her face. She shivered. *Creepy*.

Chapter 4

November 4th Afternoon

Scrolling through her contact list on her phone, Yasmin called Jessica's number. "Hey, chica. What are you doing?"

"What time is it?" Jessica groaned.

"Noon."

"Why did you wake me up so early?"

Early? Puzzled, Yasmin pulled her phone away from her ear and stared at it, as if she was expecting it to answer her question. Jessica was always up hours before she was, and then she remembered that blond guy, Ryan. "Oops. Sorry, chica. I'll call back later," she apologized.

"No, no. I'm awake now." Jessica answered. "What's up?"

"It's our day off, and I thought we could do a little treasure hunting. You know, search for pirate gold."

Naked, Jessica's feet hit the floor with an enthusiastic thump. "Hell, yes! That sounds like an outstanding idea," she agreed quickly before glancing at the bed, remembering that she wasn't alone. *Oh crap. Ryan.*

Hearing Jessica talking on the phone, Ryan turned over, grinning sleepily at her, "What's an outstanding idea? Maybe you want some more of this?" he asked, lifting the sheet to expose his revived erection.

Crushing the cell phone to her chest so that he couldn't hear what Yasmin was saying, or Yasmin hear what Ryan was asking, Jessica stammered, "Ah, no, but I had a great time last night. Gotta go do some stuff with Yasmin. You know, girl stuff."

He lifted his gaze to meet her eyes and waggled his eyebrows, "Really? Are you sure I can't interest you in a little breakfast before you go?"

Turning her back on Ryan, she muttered into her phone, "Yasmin, I have to deal with something first. Then I'll need a few more minutes to have a quick shower and toss on some clean clothes. Where do you want to meet?"

"I'm just getting out of a taxi at the Hacienda Mundaca Park," Yasmin said as she handed the driver his fare and slid out of the car. Speaking quietly, she added, "Since this is where Mundaca lived, I was thinking we should start there."

"Awesome idea. Be there in fifteen."

"Okay, good. See you soon."

Jessica tossed Ryan's pants at him, "Sorry. I gotta go. You're going to have to hustle up and clear out of here, pronto." Jessica grabbed an oversized t-shirt to cover her nakedness, shouting over her shoulder at Ryan, "No hot water. Just cold. Forget about having a shower." She really didn't want him hanging around trying to get her back into bed or tagging along when she met up with Yasmin. *They were going treasure hunting. Awesome.*

Grumbling, Ryan pulled on his pants and shirt, searched around for his sandals, and ran a hand through his short blond hair. "Hey, you want to get together tonight? Drinks and maybe something to eat? Me for dessert?"

Jessica stopped mid-stride, "Uh, not sure. Depends on how long our errands take today. What's your cell number? I'll call you later, okay?"

"That's supposed to be my line, Jessica." Annoyed, he jerked open the front door, slamming it behind him, then clomped out onto the street. "I'll call you later. Maybe," he mumbled, climbing into the back seat of a nearby taxi.

"That's supposed to be my line," Jessica said, mimicking Ryan's snotty response. "What a baby."

Waiting for Jessica to arrive, Yasmin mulled over their transportation options. Relying on the local taxi service limited their freedom. Sure, the island was only seven kilometers long, and there were over three hundred taxis providing transportation, so getting around wasn't a big problem, but if they were going treasure hunting, they needed to be careful. They didn't want people asking awkward questions.

It might be time to empty out her meager savings account and buy something for transportation. She had two affordable options, a used golf cart or a motor-scooter. There were over a thousand golf carts buzzing around the island roads on any given day. Some were privately owned, while others were available for rent by the day or the week to visiting tourists. Occasionally a used cart came up for sale, the new ones being well beyond her budget range.

On the other hand, motor-scooters, affectionately known as *motos,* were much cheaper and easier to purchase. Even the local grocery store had several in stock. Maybe she should buy one second-hand from someone who was upgrading, except locals were notoriously bad at caring for cars and motorcycles, preferring to ignore problems until the vehicles stopped functioning. She knew this from personal experience, having ridden in countless taxis with the *check engine* warning light shining like a beacon on the dashboard. Add engine oil? Why? Check the coolant level? Too much bother. Her dad had taught her the value of protecting the investment in a vehicle, but in fairness to other owners, the unrelenting humid and salty air created rust and corrosion problems that were nearly impossible to beat. Even the municipal police cruisers and city maintenance trucks were borderline dilapidated, usually only surviving four to five years in the salty environment before being consigned to the scrap heap.

Thoughts of her transportation problems evaporated as she spied Jessica arriving at the park entrance. "Let's get at it!" Jessica eagerly shouted as she hopped out of the taxi.

"Keep your voice down." Yasmin laughed while making shushing motions.

"Okay, okay. I'm pumped about the whole seventy thousand pieces of eight—however the hell much that is. Bring on the pieces of eight."

Smiling at her friend's enthusiasm, Yasmin pointed at an old stone archway and iron gates, "That's the entrance. It's hard to spot behind these other additions."

"Wow. Pretty cool place. I've never gone into the park before."

"The large palapa-covered area," Yasmin pointed up at the tall structure covering the stamped-concrete plaza, "is used for local celebrations or Zumba exercise classes. The two wings on either side were supposed to be artist studios. That didn't work out, so now some of the rooms are being used as a free animal clinic, sponsored by the Isla Animals rescue society." Sensing the presence of the women, several dogs yapped excitedly in their outside cages.

"Ah, cute," Jessica said, snapping candid images of the assorted mutts clamoring for attention.

"Come on, let's go," Yasmin said, pointing towards the entrance. At the gate, the women paid the small admission fee to the woman wearing a name tag—Adela. They waited patiently while she secured a paper wristband on their left arms as proof of payment.

Strolling in the direction of Mundaca's modest little stone house, they pretended they were sightseeing. They climbed the stone stairs leading to a concrete pathway that snaked its way past an outdoor model of an original Mayan hut, complete with life-sized figurines of a family group.

Jessica took several more photos, adding to their sightseeing cover story. "Selfie time," she shouted, pulling Yasmin closer, and snapping a photo of their two grinning faces. "Where should we start searching?" Jessica whispered as she sent the selfie to Yasmin's Instagram address.

Yasmin checked the map image on her phone, the one that Jessica had taken and shared with her the first time they looked at the document. "Well, according to this, we should be looking for something that looks like these thin wiggly lines, I guess." She lifted her head, scanning around the hacienda. Nothing looked remotely like the drawing. "Come on, let's check inside. Maybe we'll see something there."

Chapter 5

November 4th Afternoon

Inside the hacienda's stone walls were two small rooms with a few faded photographs stuck to the walls—reproductions of old etchings depicting Spanish Captains and pirates that were rumored to have visited the island in previous centuries. One sepia-colored image was labeled Francisco Fernandez de Cordoba, the Spanish conquistador credited as the first European to discover Isla Mujeres in 1517. The gloomy back room had a staircase leading up to a second floor. Jessica clambered up the steep and narrow stairs, clutching the rickety wooden railing. "Not much up here, just a tiny loft area that might have been his bedroom. I wonder if the floor is safe." She gingerly placed one foot on the termite-infested wood and tested it with her weight. "Seems okay. I'm going to have a quick peek around."

"Be careful. This place is over a hundred years old, and it hasn't been maintained very well,"

Yasmin cautioned with a grin. "It's good you are such a skinny little thing. Me, I'd crash through that old wooden floor, and that would be the end of our adventure."

Jessica scoffed, "yeah, sure. You are a regular *Gordita*, a fatty. You should probably lose that huge amount of excess weight you are carrying around. Like maybe a half a kilo, *Gordita*."

Ignoring Jessica's teasing comment, Yasmin yelled up the stairs, "See anything that looks like buried treasure? A better map? A GPS unit with the coordinates marked 'Find Pirate Treasure Here'?"

"Nope. Just a little room with a tiny window and a door. Hang on, I'll check what's on the other side of the door. Ah, it's the roof of the room below. I'll just pop out here and look." Jessica opened the door and again tested the floor with her weight. "Hey, Yasmin?"

"Si?"

"I'm going down the outside stairs, and I'll meet you at the back of the house, okay?"

"*Claro que sí,*" Yasmin agreed.

A few minutes later, Yasmin heard Jessica as she clumped down the wooden stairs. She walked around the back of the house, searching for anything unusual in the plaster-covered stone walls. *Who I am kidding?* She thought. *I haven't a clue what the heck we should be looking for*. As she rounded the corner of the house, a brief flash of red caught her peripheral vision. She scrutinized the tangled jungle of palm, papaya, and mango trees forming a dense thicket of greenery behind the building. Not seeing anything unusual, she shrugged away the uneasiness. *Probably just another tourist checking out the hacienda.*

"Whew! Hot! We should have brought some bottled water with us." Jessica brushed her hands together, dusting off bits of rotten wood dislodged from the wobbly handrail on the outside set of stairs.

"Good idea for next time."

Using the back of her hand, Jessica pushed her bangs away from her sweaty forehead. "Where next?"

"Let's try over by the lake," Yasmin pointed east across the pathway. "There are some abandoned foundations and stone walls in that area. Watch out for Alfredo, though. He's fast, and he's mean."

"Alfredo? Who's Alfredo?"

"No, not who. What. Alfredo is a big and cranky crocodile that lives in that lake with his spouse and a few of their youngsters."

"A crocodile! What the hell?" Jessica quickly scanned the ground around her feet as if she expected to see a large gap-toothed reptile preparing to latch onto her well-toned and tanned leg. "Why doesn't the municipality just get rid of him? Them? The whole damn bunch?"

Thinking Jessica's reaction was excessive and humorous, Yasmin slanted a teasing grin at her. It wasn't often that her gutsy friend was nervous about anything. "Crocodiles are native to Mexico. The locals think it's kind of cool to have a family of them on the island. It's also a great way for parents to threaten misbehaving kids, 'Be good or the crocodile will get you.'" Contorting her face, she growled. "Muhuhuh." Scanning the pathway for wayward reptiles or lurking pirates, Yasmin continued her story, "Alfredo does escape from time to time. A few years ago, he managed to find his way from the lake to the ocean on the eastern side of the island."

"Are you kidding me? Then what happened?" Theatrically shivering, Jessica peered towards the lake.

"The hunt was on. The police were notified. The municipality workers turned out in force. The Navy sent two guys with rifles. Everyone, including a crowd of about fifty locals, trailed along the eastern coastline, trying to get pictures. He was fast. By the time I heard what was happening and caught a ride with a friend, the crocodile was already swimming past the backside of the Navy base at the northern end of the island."

"How did they catch him?" The story was beginning to intrigue Jessica.

Yasmin pointed towards another pathway, "Let's head up here and see where it goes." She ran a hand over her face, trying to squeegee the sweat from her eyes, before continuing the story. "Well, three fishermen managed to toss a net over the beast and haul him into their boat. After a ton of photos with the various policía, Navy, and harbor guys pretending that they had caught him, Alfredo was put back in his lake here at the park." Yasmin stopped for a minute to peer down an abandoned well. *Nothing.* "Check my Facebook page. I posted an album labeled 'The Great Crocodile Hunt'."

"Crocodiles, what next?" grumbled Jessica as she trudged along the gravel pathway. "And besides, why call it Alfredo? If you are going to name the evil bastard, name him Carlos after our boss or César after the guy that was lurking around the bar last month, but not Alfredo. Alfredo is a better name for an alligator."

A smile quirked Yasmin's lips, "There are no alligators in Mexico. They only live in the USA or China. I don't know what the crocodile's name is. I just named him Alfredo to tease one of my cousins,

Freddy. Besides, I think Carlos Mendoza is hot." Just the thought of him made her heart tap dance a little.

And there it was again, that quick flash of red off to one side. Puzzled, Yasmin turned to Jessica, "Hey, did you see anything odd just now?"

"What?"

"Like someone hiding in the bushes? Running from one hiding place to another?"

Slowly turning in a circle, Jessica tried to spot what Yasmin was fussing about. "Nope, I don't see anything." Grinning, she teased, "Were you drinking Absinthe last night? That stuff can make you see things for sure."

"*Mierda.* I don't touch that stuff," she almost gagged at the memory of the one and only time that she had sampled the infamous French liquor, recently made legal again after being banned for over a hundred years in most countries because of its rumored hallucinogenic properties. She had definitely been seeing things that night—a dark smoky mist drifting through the streets. *Never again.* Yasmin shuddered involuntarily. "No, really, I swear I saw something—just now. Like a person wearing something red and darting through the bushes. Weird."

"It's all this talk about crocodiles. You're seeing things."

It took another hour of searching derelict foundations, peering into abandoned wells, and inching cautiously along the shoreline of the lake while watching for the crocodiles before the women were ready to admit defeat for the day. The warm, salty air was heavy with the intoxicating scent of bougainvillea and Mexican plumeria, *Flores de Mayo*. A few gnarled, abandoned fruit trees struggled in the thin layer of soil covering the limestone and sand foundation of the island. The stingless Yucatan honeybees droned sleepily in the late afternoon sun. If it weren't for the mosquitoes, Yasmin thought, this would have been a very pleasant location for a hacienda.

Dirty, hot, and bug bitten, they retraced their steps to the entrance gates. "Gawd, I need a drink." Jessica plumped down on a concrete bench, stretching her back muscles and twisting her neck from side to side.

Discouraged, Yasmin dropped onto the bench beside Jessica, "We barely covered a quarter of the park. There are still the caves and the secret garden area, plus the rest of the hot, mosquito-infested jungle to tromp through."

"Yeah, well, I'm done for the day," Jessica stood up, stretching her arms overhead. "Let's head home, get cleaned up, and find something to eat, preferably something jammed with calories. And cold beer. I need at least a dozen frosty Sols. Ummm. My kind of diet."

"Uff. I hate you. All you do is eat and drink, and you are still a *mujercita flaca,* a skinny little bitch."

"Hey, watch that," Jessica playfully slapped Yasmin's arm, "*Gordita*."

Chapter 6

November 4th Evening

Yasmin turned the key in the lock and pushed open her front door. She tossed her large purse on the kitchen counter and then opened the refrigerator, sadly surveying its non-existent meal choices. "Nothing but wine and beer. Should we order in?"

"Yep, good idea."

"Pizza?"

"Try that new place just down the street. I've heard it's great."

Yasmin flipped through the pile of food delivery flyers stuffed into her mailbox on a regular basis. Amazing how many home delivery options there were for food on the island. There had to be at least a dozen. Pizza seemed to be a favorite home-delivery staple in Mexico, right up there with tacos. Pulling a colorful leaflet out from the stack, she waved it overhead, "Got it. A large thin-crust pizza split down the middle, half vegetarian for me and half loaded for you. Right?"

"Sounds good."

Waiting for their food to arrive, Jessica took a long slow swig of an icy cold Sol and then settled back in the comfortably padded chair. Thumbing through the internet on her phone, she brought up the Wikipedia page for de Graaf. "So, this pirate guy, the cute one, Lorencillo de Graaf—did he hide the treasure back in the 1680s on the same property where Mundaca built his house? Or did he hide it someplace else, and Mundaca moved it to his property? I don't get it."

"I'm not sure either. I guess he found it on his property," Yasmin answered as she studied the photo on her phone, trying to decipher the squiggly lines of what appeared to be a map. Shoreline? Caves? Not even the slightest idea of what it was supposed to be. The letter held a clue that just wouldn't reveal itself, and she just couldn't leave it alone. "It does seem a bit odd that de Graaf would hike inland with his heavy treasure just to bury it. I'd have thought he could find a safe location closer to where he anchored."

Reaching across the table, Yasmin picked up a bottle of Salentein Argentinian Malbec and tipped a bit of the rich red wine into her glass. It was expensive, but since she drank so little, she occasionally treated herself to the good stuff. She glanced at Jessica, tilting the bottle towards her. "You want some of this wine? It's really tasty." Jessica shook her head, pointing at her bottle of beer. "And, what do you mean, the cute one?" Yasmin asked.

"Lorencillo-baby. I just Googled him." She pointed at her phone, "It says here that he was quite the ladies' man, a swordsman if you know what I mean. Wink, wink, nudge, nudge." Jessica grinned lasciviously, "His real name was Laurens Cornelis Boudewijn de Graaf. Lorencillo was his nickname. He was rumored to be a very successful pirate, richer than Blackbeard or Captain Kidd. Married at least twice, he was tall and blond, and very handsome. He could play both a violin and trumpet, and he could recite his favorite Shakespearean play, King Lear, from memory in two languages." She fanned her face with a hand. "It makes me hot just to read about him."

"Jeesh, you're like a cat in heat around men." Yasmin teased without looking up from the map.

"I'm a scorching hot mamma cat, looking for a handsome new tom-cat." Jessica struck a mock sexy pose—head back, chest out—then laughed as she relaxed back into a normal posture. "Besides, fantasizing about handsome pirates is harmless fun." A slight grimace of disappointment crossed her face as she continued to read the results of her internet browsing, "I don't think we can count on the entire seventy thousand pieces of eight to be stashed on Isla."

Intrigued, Yasmin stopped obsessing over the map and looked up at Jessica. "Really? Why?"

"Because it says here that the pirate crews always shared the treasure. As far back as when these guys were alive there were what was known as articles of agreement. It's a set of rules for each ship, governing code of conduct, punishments for infractions, and how many shares of the plunder each crew member would receive."

Jessica took a small sip of beer and continued reading aloud the internet article. "The captains and quartermasters typically received one-and-a-half to two shares of the entire amount of the loot. Crew members with more skills—such as doctors, carpenters, and gunners—were given about one-and-a-half shares. All other able-bodied seamen were entitled to one share. There was even a common share that was held for seriously injured members." She glanced over at Yasmin, "That's surprisingly democratic when you think about it."

"So, we really don't have any idea of how much, if anything, he buried on Isla."

Jessica shook her head, "Nope, not a clue, but trying to solve this three-hundred-year-old mystery is fun, and I sort of like Lorencillo. He sounds like he was a bit of a gentleman, about some things at least."

"A gentleman? Really?"

"Yep, he had a falling out with two of the other pirate captains that were involved with the siege at Veracruz. It was over the handling of their hostages. Michel de Grammont planned to execute the captives who couldn't pay the ransom for their release. Lorencillo disagreed, and they parted company. Then his countryman, Van Hoorn, beheaded a few of the prisoners to apply pressure for the ransom payments. Lorencillo de Graaf challenged him to a sword fight. De Graaf won the duel and prevented the murder of more of the captives. So, yeah, sort of a pirate-gentleman." She fiddled with the now-empty bottle of beer.

Yasmin smiled, thinking Jessica had, at times, an unusual set of values. Curious about what Jessica thought of Ryan, she asked, "What about that guy you were with at *El Arrecife*? What happened to him?"

"Oh, he's okay. Not sure I want to pursue that one any further, though." Deftly plaiting her long blond hair into a fat, loose braid, Jessica flipped the thick pigtail over her shoulder, letting it settle in the center of her back. She stood up and opened Yasmin's fridge, searching for another beer.

"Why? Don't you like him?"

Twisting the cap off the cold Sol, Jessica shrugged non-committedly, trying to deflect Yasmin's question. "He's a bit pushy, asking tons of questions about that piece of paper. 'What was it? Where did you find it?' Yadda, yadda, yadda." She grinned, "But the sex was pretty good, so, maybe I'll see him again. We'll see."

Surprised by Jessica's admission that Ryan had been quizzing her about the piece of paper, Yasmin accidentally jostled a bit of wine from her glass onto the table, just missing her smartphone. "He asked you about the letter?" She reached for a few pieces of paper towel to mop up the wine, "What did you tell him?" she anxiously probed.

A voice called from outside her door, "Señorita Yasmin? Pizza."

"Hey, pizza's here." Jessica said, hopping up to pay for their delivery.

Settled with their slices and drinks, Yasmin picked right back up on their conversation before they had been interrupted by the arrival of their food. Jessica was avoiding eye contact; she looked like she didn't want to answer the question. "What did you tell Ryan about the letter?"

Her eyes glancing to the left, Jessica replied "Nothing. I just told him the same story you told him. It was a note from your grandmother asking you to visit her. But he just wouldn't leave it alone." She busied herself with taking another piece of the pizza.

"Um, Jessica. Remember I mentioned I thought I saw someone running through the bushes at the hacienda? Do you think he followed us?"

"How would he know where we were going?" Jessica looked quizzically at Yasmin.

"He was at your house this morning. Did you actually see him leave your neighborhood?"

"No, not exactly." Her eyebrows crunched together as she set the bottle down on the table. "I heard a car door slam. I assumed he had gotten into a taxi and headed back to his place. Maybe we're just being paranoid."

"Yeah, maybe." Pushing away her suspicions, Yasmin shrugged, no sense getting tangled up in what ifs, at this point. "So tomorrow, should we search for a few hours in the morning? We don't have to be at work until four in the afternoon."

"Yep. It will be cooler in the morning that's for sure. You gonna be able to get up and be ready by the time the park opens at nine?"

Yasmin swatted playfully at her friend, "Of course. I'm going to bed as soon as you leave." Yawning, she stretched her arms up, and then lowered them slowly behind her shoulders, feeling a satisfying pull on her muscles. Yasmin shook out her shoulders and arms, then pointed at the leftovers. "Take some pizza home with you in case you get hungry. I'm done. I need a shower and my bed."

Chapter 7

November 5th Afternoon

Yasmin rubbed a wet cloth across the granite bar top, cleaning up the sticky drink residue left by recent patrons. The *Loco Lobo* was a great place to work, with Carlos as a fun but unflappable boss. The restaurant was decorated in what he humorously referred to as single-guy chic, with dark wooden ceiling beams, stamped-concrete floors, and a masculine color scheme of black, cobalt blue and lime green. Large pictures, courtesy of local photographer Tony Garcia, adorned three walls. The photos depicted the colorful open-deck, *panga* fishing boats, fishermen repairing their nets when the ocean was too rough for working, and the faces of old islanders weathered by time and hard work. The fourth wall wasn't really a wall, but an intricate metal security gate that rolled up and out of the way, allowing the restaurant to literally spill out into the street with additional tables and chairs.

The open and airy space of the *Loco Lobo* was one of the most popular places on the island for good bar food and generous drinks. Still it was the same thing, every day. Pour drinks and serve customers. Sometimes the tourists' casual generalizations and rude comments about Mexicans really got under her skin, especially the comments that started with "They..." as in *they* do this, or *they* do that, as if all Mexicans behaved in an identical manner. Then there were the visitors who wouldn't attempt to learn even a few polite words of Spanish.

But the tips were good, and she really liked working with Carlos and Jessica, so she stayed. Maybe, just maybe, this fantasy of finding the pirates' loot would come true. Dreams were nice, but that didn't put food in her tummy or pay the rent.

They had spent their morning trudging around the secret garden at the Hacienda Mundaca Park but hadn't got any closer to finding the treasure. True the gardens were beautiful. Stone benches lined the hexagonal perimeter. Fading lines of poetry carved into stone archways were still faintly visible. Jewel-toned flowering vines climbed over abandoned walls and the fruit trees were laden with ripening papayas and mangos. They still didn't have any idea of where to look, or even if the treasure was actually hidden there. Maybe it had been found by another local who had managed to keep the discovery quiet. That would be a huge let-down if they were searching for something that didn't exist.

At the end of this morning's four-hour search, she still didn't know if pieces of eight were made of gold or silver, and how much the treasure might be worth. If the Mexican government got wind of what they were doing...well, who knew how much trouble they would be in. As a national she was controlled by the laws of the country and she could end up in jail while the mess got sorted out. Jessica, a foreigner on a work permit, was also governed by Mexican law, but would hopefully be deported back to Canada and not jailed. The legal system in Mexico was different than what most foreigners were accustomed to. Here when people were arrested, they stayed in jail until they could prove their innocence and a trial didn't necessarily happen quickly. She knew of one island man who had been accused—wrongly it turned out—of sexually assaulting a young woman. He languished in jail for over two years before he was proven innocent and released.

A ripple of apprehension trembled through her body. Somehow, she had to find out the law concerning found treasure without tipping their hand as to what they were up to. *Google it? Maybe? Ask a local notario about the laws?* But that might make the person curious about her reasons for asking for the information. *Who could she trust?*

"A peso for your thoughts," teased Jessica, smiling at Yasmin, "and I need two margaritas no salt, four freaking cold Sols and a mojito for table four." She set her large serving tray on the counter, in preparation for the new drink order.

Shifting her concentration back to her job, Yasmin said, "Okay got it."

"It's busy today, but not crazy busy." Jessica lingered at the bar, straightening the container of colored swizzle sticks and the pile of cocktail napkins while she waited for the drink order to be filled.

"I like it. Makes the day go quicker." Yasmin replied as she cast a quick glance towards the pedestrians-only street. A steady procession of selfie-stick toting tourists paraded by, their chins tilted upwards as they grinned inanely for the camera. The sidewalk tables were filled with sunburnt and scantily clad vacationers of every body type, some that definitely shouldn't be scantily clad in public. People on vacation were typically more relaxed about their appearances. *Whatever makes them happy*, she mused.

Jessica said, "Seriously though, why the long face?"

"Just thinking about our situation. Thinking about the legality of what we are doing." Yasmin's deft hands quickly assembled the drink order and slid the brimming margarita glasses towards Jessica.

Jessica settled the drinks and the four beers on her serving platter, waiting until the mojito was finished before lifting the tray into a one-handed position near her right shoulder. "Legal-smegal. Let's see if we can find it first, then worry about that other stuff," she laughed, spinning gracefully and heading towards her customers.

Yasmin noticed the door to Carlos' tiny ground-floor office opening. It must be time for his mid-afternoon rounds of the restaurant. He liked to chat with customers several times during business hours, giving people a sense that their business was appreciated. He wove his way around the tables and chairs, stopping frequently to shake hands with acquaintances or greet strangers, gradually making his way over to where Yasmin was working.

"Hi Yasmin, everything going okay?" Even with a beaming smile, the faint scar on his face gave him the don't-mess-with-me look of a streetwise tough guy. He was fit, and if pushed wouldn't walk away from a fight, but he was a good friend and Yasmin trusted him.

"Can I ask you a question, Carlos?" She asked as his delicious, dark chocolate-colored eyes searched her face, causing her pulse to flutter.

"Of course, what is it?" He leaned against the nearby wall, arms overlapping across his chest, one leg crossed comfortably over the other.

"Do you have a local *notario* you use? Someone honest, and not too expensive?" She continued setting up drink orders, trying to act casual, like her question was no big deal.

"Sure, Luis Aguilar, on the corner of Juarez and Matamoros."

"Okay, that's great. Thanks." She shot him a quick smile and turned away from his curious gaze.

"Why do you need legal advice?" His eyebrows knotted together in concern, "is there something I can help you with?"

Avoiding his searching looks, Yasmin kept her back turned as she restocked the beer refrigerator. "It's nothing really, just a couple of questions for my *abuela*, about her land in Valladolid." Mentally crossing her fingers, she hoped her grandmother didn't mind that she was using her as a cover for her many lies. *My apologies Abuelita; I'll go to confession tomorrow.* And then she realized she couldn't go to confession. Not tomorrow. Not the next day. Maybe not ever again. How could she confess to her local priest that she was illegally treasure hunting?

Chapter 8

November 6th Early afternoon

Yasmin pushed open the door of the orange-painted building on the corner of Matamoros and Juarez, the office of Notario 42, Luis Aguilar. She was feeling confident, having taken a bit more effort with her clothing and makeup for this meeting, adding a light touch of *Glam* perfume to her wrists. Mentally crossing her fingers, she hoped this wasn't a big mistake, asking for information on the legality of treasure hunting. Hopefully, he would believe her story about researching for a proposed novel.

Inside the cool air-conditioned room, a woman sat behind a desk just large enough to hold a telephone, a laptop computer and a stack of files that she was obviously working through. Her desk name plate said Yolanda Rincale. Greeting Yasmin with a smile that spread across her face and lit up her large brown eyes, she asked how they could help her today. Yasmin introduced herself and said she had an appointment with the *notario*.

"Ah yes, of course." Señora Rincale held up a finger, "Momentito, por favor," and pressed the button to connect to her boss. A few words, and a head nod, she disconnected the call. "Señor Aguilar will see you now Señorita Medina," the receptionist said as she indicated the door on the right.

"Gracias," said Yasmin, her heels lightly clicking on the marble-tiled floor as she maneuvered past the receptionist and into the inner office. "Buenos Dias Señor Aguilar," she said, thinking Jessica would be licking her lips over this guy. Slim and athletically built, he looked like he was a serious runner, with short well-trimmed hair, long lean muscles, and not a scrap of extra body fat visible. He was impeccably dressed in well-tailored pants and a turquoise-colored *guayabera*, the favorite short-sleeved linen shirt worn by local businessmen, plus the ever-present, over-sized expensive watch recently so popular with men.

Walking around his desk, Luis reached out to lightly touch Yasmin's hand in a respectful Mayan greeting. "Buenos Dias Señorita Medina. What can I do for you today?" he asked, motioning her towards the two client chairs in front of his desk.

Folding her long slim legs demurely under the chair, Yasmin regarded the *notario* quietly for a minute. It was odd in a way on an island this small that she had never met Luis Aguilar before, but with sixteen thousand people living and working on Isla, sometimes there were people you just never bumped into. She had seen him a time or two chatting with Carlos on the street but had never been introduced to him, and without an introduction, the traditional warm Latino greeting of a light hug and a kiss on the cheek was considered to be too informal a gesture.

"I have a few questions that might sound a bit strange, but I was hoping you could help me with a project I am working on."

"Okay," He rolled his hand in a *please continue talking* gesture.

Yasmin fiddled with her purse, "Well, you see, I am working on a novel about a woman who finds a treasure, a pirate's treasure actually, and I need advice to make the book more authentic."

"Ah, a novelist." Aguilar smiled indulgently, his deep brown eyes crinkling with amusement. "What do you need to know?"

"If the main character finds the treasure, will she be allowed to keep it?"

"Good question. I have no idea." Luis grinned, leaning back in his leather chair while he considered her question. "It's not a common legal problem as I am sure you realize."

"Yes, of course. I shouldn't have bothered you with this." Embarrassed at wasting his time, Yasmin started to stand up, but Aguilar motioned her to stay seated.

"No, no. Don't worry. I didn't say I wouldn't help you. I just said it is not a common legal problem." He leaned forward and made a note in his organizer. "Give me a day or two, I will find the answer for you."

"Oh, I see. Thank you."

"Now tell me more about the book. Where will the treasure be found? On land or in the ocean? And which country did it come from? England? Spain? France?" Aguilar's eyes twinkled with amusement. "That might make a difference as to legal ownership of the hoard."

"Oh, I hadn't thought of those complications. Perhaps you could do a little research for all those options? That way I can adjust the story so that my character can keep the treasure." Reaching into her purse, Yasmin pulled out several one hundred peso banknotes, "Could you please tell me how much that would cost?"

Waving away her offer of cash, Aguilar smiled, "No need to pay me in advance. I know you work for my friend Carlos. Come back Friday, I should have an answer then."

Clutching the sheaf of pesos in her hand, Yasmin's eyebrows scrunched together in worry. "Ah, Señor Aguilar, I am a bartender. I don't have a lot of money so I would like to put a limit on how much I spend."

"Okay, no problem." He drummed his pen on his desk, thinking for a moment, "How about one thousand pesos? Would that work for you?"

Less than a hundred dollars. I can afford that. "That is very generous of you Señor Aguilar. Thank you so much."

"De nada. And please call me Luis. Señor Aguilar is my father." He smiled again, "Perhaps when your novel is finished you can mention me in the author's acknowledgements—you know the part where the writer thanks everyone from her kindergarten teacher all the way up to her proofing editor, and maybe even her hairstylist for contributing to the novel."

"Absolutely. I will also give you a complimentary copy, signed by me," Yasmin agreed. *Another lie. Another sin.*

Chapter 9

November 7th Morning

Luis Aguilar tapped his pen on his desk in time to the soft salsa music leaking out of his iPod; music helped him think. After a few hours researching in various legal manuals and on-line documents, he'd discovered that Mexican law forbids searching for lost treasure in the oceans without a Mexican federal permit. *Okay, good.* So, Yasmin's fictitious treasure-hunter could apply for a federal permit. *Yeah, not quite so easy.* There were no records for any permit ever, in the history of Mexico, being granted to search for treasure. So basically, it was an impossible situation.

However, on land, that was a slightly different story, as the federal mineral rights started at one meter deep, so theoretically if the treasure was found in the top one meter of earth, the treasure-hunter could keep the bullion. Theoretically. It also depended on who owned the land that was one meter above the federal mineral rights. The landowner was entitled to keep the treasure found on his or her land. Ayieee! No clear answer on this one either.

Further research revealed that many of the countries bordering on the Caribbean Sea paid a ten-percent finder's fee to anyone who located an ancient treasure. This was to encourage privately funded searches in hopes of locating historic ships lost to storms, or to pirates and buccaneers. But he couldn't find any record of Mexico paying out the ten percent. Instead he read with great interest the unlucky saga of the Veracruz fisherman, Raúl Hurtado, who discovered what was referred to as *The Fisherman's Jewels*.

In 1975, while searching for octopus in the shallow waters of a reef, *Coral de Enmedio*, Hurtado noticed a glint of gold in the wave-swept sand. It was a gold ingot.

Returning to the same location at a later date, he discovered more artifacts, including forty-two Aztec gold pieces, jewels, bracelets, and clothing ornaments. Uneducated, Hurtado was unaware that he was legally obligated to report the find to the government. He also had no knowledge of the worth of the items that he had found. His children played on the beach, dragging a line of gold ingots on a string—shiny playthings that were temporarily amusing. Hurtado did cash in a small item or two to pay for a new tin roof on the family's modest casita. Eventually, the authorities got wind of the discovery, and Hurtado was jailed on a charge of looting federal property. It was a full year before he was acquitted by the Mexican Supreme Court in 1979.

Whew, Luis thought. *The Fisherman's Jewels* was a fascinating story, but it was unimaginable how aggravating it had been for Raúl Hurtado. The impoverished man had found millions in lost treasure, only to be summarily thrown into prison for not reporting it. According to the follow-up story in 2013 by Fox News Latino, the same fisherman was in danger of being ousted from his humble home in the harbor of Veracruz because it was in the path of expansion plans for the harbor. Amazing. Some people have nothing but bad luck.

Turning his attention back to Yasmin's original questions, Luis' fingers danced lightly over the computer keyboard, composing a short summary of his findings. He hit the print button and the information spooled from the computer to the printer. No need to bother his assistant, Yolanda, for such a small task.

Slipping the letter into a large envelope, he licked and sealed the flap. *Well, then,* he mused, *Yasmin has a real dilemma to solve for her fictitious character. Will the treasure be in the ocean or on land? Will she keep the treasure or have to turn it over to the authorities?* He reached for his phone, thumbing the contact number for Carlos.

Leaning back in his chair, he crossed his right leg comfortably over his left knee, waiting until Carlos answered. He absently plucked at his pant leg, ensuring the cloth settled smoothly on his well-toned leg. *Good clothes made the man*, his father had told him time and again, especially when you are a businessman. Luis enjoyed the feel of expensive slacks, good leather shoes, and linen shirts. God only knew how he would afford his lifestyle if he ever did get married. "Hey bud, how's it hanging?"

"Luis, you over-charging gangster, how're you doing?"

"Good, man, really good. I have a bit of information for Yasmin when you see her."

"Ah, okay," Carlos hesitated, "but isn't this confidential lawyer-client information?"

"No, it's nothing important. It's just a bit of info she was looking for about Mexican laws and treasure hunting."

"Treasure hunting?" Unseen by Luis, Carlos scratched his head. "That's weird."

"Yep. Apparently, she's a wannabe novelist and needs information about ownership of buried treasure. I told her to come back Friday, but I have the information for her now if she wants to drop by."

"Okay, gracias. She's due in this afternoon at four, but I can call her and ask her to stop by your office on the way to work."

"Great. Next time the *cerveza* is on you. *Muchas cervezas.*"

"Why do I owe *you* free beers?"

"Because I was fast, and I gave her a good price."

"*Pendejo!*" Carlos laughed as he disconnected the call.

He hit the speed dial for Yasmin's cell phone, listening to it ring until the voicemail option kicked in. "Yasmin, this is Carlos. Luis Aguilar called. He has the information you requested. You can drop by his office on your way to work. See you at four, chica," he added with a smile in his voice. "Don't be late."

Chapter 10

November 7th Early afternoon

Listening to the voicemail message from Carlos, Yasmin nibbled on her bottom lip, wondering if Luis Aguilar had said anything about her interest in the treasure laws. In a small community like Isla, it was inevitable that personal info was nonchalantly exchanged. A chat with a close friend typically became part of another casual conversation between other friends, and before you knew it, it seemed like the entire community knew your business. *Notario* or not, Luis had likely mentioned something to Carlos. It was the downside of living in a tight-knit society where people deeply cared about their families and neighbors.

Glancing at her phone, she realized she had to get moving if she wanted to stop by the law office and still get to work on time—no sense in irritating Carlos by being late yet again.

Hopping first on one foot and then the other, she tightened the straps of her favorite red stiletto heels. They were murder to wear for nine hours bartending or waitressing, but they were killer-good shoes for getting big tips. Jessica called them *fuck me shoes*. Crude but true. The male customers liked to ogle their legs and butts and always tipped more when the women wore sexy high heels. *Sex sells most anything that men want,* she thought, *alcohol, or expensive cars, or big boats—toys for boys.*

Yasmin gathered up her keys, phone, and sunglasses. She locked her front door and moved to the sidewalk, waiting in front of her casita for an available taxi to cruise her street. A quick toot on a horn alerted her that the driver had room for another customer.

Greeting the two other passengers in the taxi, Yasmin settled into the backseat and pulled out her phone. She rapidly scrolled through Facebook, thumbing in "like" or "love" responses to friends' recent posts. Checking incoming Instagram messages, then flipping over to Twitter, she was caught up on her social life by the time the taxi stopped in front of Luis Aguilar's office. Sliding out of the rear curbside door, she thanked the driver as she handed over the fare.

Inside the office of the *notario,* his receptionist greeted her politely as she held out an envelope for Yasmin, adding, "Señor Aguilar had an appointment this afternoon. He asked me to give you this envelope."

"Thank you, very much." Yasmin slit open the sealed legal-sized envelope and pulled out several pieces of paper.

"There is a cover letter from Señor Aguilar," said the receptionist. "It gives you a quick summary of his findings as well as the other relevant information that he printed for you. If you have any questions, he said to feel free to call him later this evening or tomorrow morning."

"Muchas gracias. Do I owe any more money?" Yasmin quickly skimmed the letter, stopping abruptly when she read the part about the fisherman going to jail for not reporting his find. Her heart hammered in her chest. *Oh my goodness, that poor man.*

"No, nothing more."

Distracted by the unbelievably tragic story of Raúl Hurtado discovering such great wealth, only to have it confiscated from him by the authorities, Yasmin mumbled a polite reply. "Gracias. Adios." Exiting the building, she started walking in the direction of Hidalgo Avenue, towards the *Loco Lobo*.

Reading as she walked, she relied on her peripheral vision to keep from bumping into the clusters of visitors milling in the downtown streets. *No different than texting and walking*, she thought.

Between the gift stores, restaurants and bars, every store front had someone hawking goods to the tourists. Two for one margaritas today. Blue light special. "Coldest beer on the island," or "Cheaper than Walmart" were the common come-on lines that she heard. The afternoon sun beat down on the paving stones, evaporating small puddles of rain left over from an earlier five-minute downpour that had been localized in the downtown area. The official end of the hurricane season was still a couple of weeks away, and the weather in early November was still variable—hot and rainy, or hot and sunny. The less humid winter season that started in December was the beginning of the tourist high season.

Finished with reading, Yasmin stuffed the papers back into the envelope. They had a problem, a big problem. They were legally obliged to advise the authorities if they found the treasure. If they didn't, and the officials got wind of the discovery, they would likely end up in prison. Forcing a relaxed expression onto her face, she strode into the *Loco Lobo*, waving at Carlos and pointing at the time displayed on her iPhone. "See, I'm early for a change," she said.

He smiled as he walked towards her, "Si, chica, for a change, you are early." Noticing the legal-sized envelope in her hand he quietly asked, "Did Luis help you with your questions?"

"Yes, he did. Thank you so much for recommending him." She snugged the long ties for her bar apron twice around her slender waist, tying the ends in a bow over her flat stomach. "He was very pleasant and helpful." Pretending to be unconcerned, she casually ignored his questioning stare.

"So, a writer?"

Flushing, Yasmin flicked a glance at Carlos, then looked away. "Well, not exactly a writer, but I have an idea for a mystery novel and thought it would be good to get my facts straight before I spend a lot of time working on it." She shrugged like it was no big deal. "No point in writing a bunch of stuff that isn't accurate."

"Yes, that's true. Well, congratulations. I am proud to know an author." Carlos' smile was warm, but if she had really looked at him, she would have realized his expression reflected amused skepticism. "Okay, then," he slapped the bar counter in a fake hearty manner and strode towards his office. "Let's get to work and make some money."

Oh damn, now she was lying to Carlos as well as Luis Aguilar, plus those two dorks Ryan and Kirk. She really was going to burn in hell or maybe end up in jail before all this was over. As Yasmin turned to fill the first drink order of her afternoon shift, she noticed Jessica breezing into the bar with the vigor of a sprinter. *Where does she get all that energy?* "Hey Jessica," she called in greeting.

Jessica stopped mid-stride. Crossing her hands over her heart, she looked shocked. "Yasmin, is that you?" She fumbled to check the time on her phone, "It's only a quarter to four."

"Yep, it's me."

"No, it can't be Yasmin. You are an imposter. What have you done with my friend Yasmin?" Jessica ducked behind the bar and opened the door on the storage area, yelling. "Yasmin! Yasmin, are you in there? There is an alien out here calling herself Yasmin."

Laughing, Yasmin flicked an olive towards her friend, "Just. Shut. Up." Jessica had a naturally buoyant personality that could lighten anyone's spirits.

"So, why the hell are you so early?" Jessica asked.

"I had to pick up some information on the way into work. I just found out we legally won't be able to keep anything we find," Yasmin whispered to Jessica.

"What? What do you mean?" Jessica whispered back tensely, "How did you find out?"

"I asked a local *notario*. Told him I was writing a novel and wanted to verify the information before I wrote the story."

"Wow. You are getting good at this covert stuff," she murmured. "So, what do we do now?"

Mixing a margarita for another server, Yasmin stopped mid-motion and pensively set the drink down on the bar. "I think we should cross that bridge when we come to it. Let's not worry about *what ifs* for now." She gave Jessica a worried smile, just a fleeting flicker on her lips. "We don't even know if the buried treasure that the pirate Fermin Mundaca found still exists. He was very ill with syphilis when he died in Mérida. Maybe he cashed in the booty to pay for living and medical expenses."

Chapter 11

November 8th Early morning

Haunted by alternating dreams of successfully finding the treasure and then nightmares of being jailed in a federal prison, Yasmin abandoned the idea of sleep. Unwinding the tangled sheets from her feet, she eased out of bed at seven in the morning. That was an almost-record-breaking time for her to be up.

She wandered into the kitchen, reaching for the coffee maker. Caffeine. She needed caffeine. Or as Jessica called it, brain-food. Spooning the last of her ground coffee into the drip-pot, she leaned against the kitchen counter to wait for the pot to finish its gurgling. When it was done, she opened her tiny refrigerator, pulling out a small container of milk whose best-before-date was teetering on the edge of not-usable. She sniffed the milk, *probably okay for today*. "I really have to get groceries," she muttered to herself.

Coffee in hand, Yasmin sat at her small table, checking for recent messages before signing into her online bank account. Nodding at the numbers displayed on the screen, she saw she could afford a motor-scooter. She relished the idea of independence, of being able to go where and when she liked.

Should she ask Jessica to help pick out a *moto*? Thinking about that for a moment or two, Yasmin decided she was capable of making her own decisions on how to spend her own money. But Jessica was fun to spend time with, so sure, why not call her?

She pushed a few buttons on her phone, then waited as the call connected. "Hey, Jess, are you up?"

"Of course. What's happening?"

"I'm going to buy a *moto* this morning. Do you want to come with me?"

"Yep! I'm always game for spending someone's money," Jessica paused, then added, "You do know how to drive a moto, right?"

"Sure, *papi* taught us when we were teenagers. It's easy."

"Okay, good. Where and when do you want to meet?"

"I still need to shower and get dressed. So, Chedraui in thirty?"

"Really? Not Yamaha or Honda?"

"No, too expensive for my budget. The *motos* at the Chedraui grocery store are cheaper. Meet me just inside the entrance doors on the lower level."

"Okay, see you there."

At the store, the motion-detector slid the glass doors open, allowing Yasmin to enter the cooler, air-conditioned space. Jessica was already standing inside.

"Okay, decision time." Jessica said, pointing at the display. "What color do you like? Red, green, blue or black? What motor size, 125cc or 150cc? And do you want an automatic or manual shift?"

Yasmin looked around and said, "More importantly, where is the salesperson?"

Riding the up-escalator to the main part of the store, Yasmin stepped off the moving-sidewalk surface, turning left towards the customer service desk. "Do you have someone who can assist me with a moto purchase?"

"Si, of course. Wait just a moment please."

Listening to the repeated requests over the in-store public address system for a salesperson to report to the customer service desk, Yasmin gave up waiting and returned to where the motos were parked. After reading the information stickers on the bikes listing features and prices, Yasmin said to Jessica, "Red is my favorite color" as she pointed at a crimson red *Italika.* "Automatic is best for me, because it's easier to drive on our busy streets" she added. "And the motor size, I don't care one way or the other as long as the price is within my budget."

The clerk finally appeared, scurrying down the escalator towards Yasmin. His employee identification tag flapped loosely on a chain hung around his neck. "Hi, my name is Alberto. How can I help you?"

Yasmin pointed, "I'd like to buy that moto, please."

"Good choice. Nice bike for the price." He agreed. "But first, please come back upstairs with me," Alberto requested, "I have to write an invoice for the moto." Gesturing to various areas of the store, he continued, "Then you have to take the invoice to the cashier and pay. Once you have paid, take the receipt to the security guard at the top of the escalator."

Yasmin nodded, agreeing that she understood. She turned towards the escalator. "Wait, please," he said, his hand upright like a traffic cop, "I'm not finished." Standing behind the salesperson, out of his line of sight, Jessica did an exaggerated eye-roll, mouthing *are you kidding me?*

Biting her top lip to stifle a giggle, Yasmin listened as Alberto continued his recital of instructions, "The security guard will write the receipt number, and pertinent information in his ledger. Then you sign and print your name in the ledger, and then," he said as he jingled the ring of keys, "I will unlock the moto for you."

Twenty long minutes later Yasmin had possession of her purchase. "What about gas?" she asked, lifting the seat and inspecting the empty gas tank.

"No, no gas." Alberto smiled pleasantly, "You'll have to go to the gas station and buy some, then come back for your moto." Yasmin groaned inwardly. Nothing was ever easy; it was always an exercise in patience. Extreme patience.

Jessica broke out in laughter. "So, you don't need to show proof that you actually have a driver's license, but you do need to provide your own gas to get it home."

"Si, isn't this fun?" Yasmin deadpanned. *Grocery shopping was going to have to wait for another day.*

The next thirty minutes were swiftly consumed with solving the no-gas problem. Yasmin dashed back into the store to purchase a plastic gas can, considering and then dismissing the idea of purchasing milk and coffee for her morning kick-start. Back on the street, they hailed a taxi for a ride to the closest gas station. The taxi driver waited while the pump-jockey filled the four-liter plastic container, then drove them back to the store. Finally, she was in possession of her new moto, with gas.

On the way to her house they stopped at a little hardware store, tucked into *Las Glorias* colonia, and Yasmin bought two matching red helmets.

Outside the store, Yasmin handed one to Jessica, "Here you go, your very own brain-bucket."

"Really, do I have to wear this? It's too hot."

"Yes, you do. They are mandatory for anyone on a moto who is over the age of six," she said, buckling her chinstrap, "and certainly we qualify."

Jessica loosely held the headgear in her hand. "But I've seen lots of bareheaded riders on the island."

"True, the helmet law has only been in effect for a few years, and people are still resisting it, especially the young guys who don't want to crush their fancy hairstyles. They usually hold the helmet up over their heads and steer with one hand. It's a bit comical actually."

"No kidding," Jessica said, with a laugh in her voice.

Yasmin mounted the moto, "Other riders protest by using an assortment of plastic pails, ice cream buckets, or construction hats as a helmet. For now, the police are ignoring the mavericks, but that could change" she said, tapping her head with a finger, and then pointing at Jessica's head.

"Okay, okay. I'll wear the stupid thing," Jessica grumbled as she strapped on her helmet.

Now, parked tight against her front steps, Yasmin ran a possessive hand over the shiny paint of the *Italika*. "Pretty."

Jessica nodded, agreeing with Yasmin's assessment of her new plaything. "Yep, pretty. You'll have a lot of fun with this little baby." Looking at the back of the scooter, Jessica added, "There's no licence plate."

"No worries, I have thirty days to licence the moto."

"Okay, good," Jessica said, checking the time on her phone, "We still have a few hours before we have to be at work. I'm thinking we should do a little reconnaissance and see if we can figure out where Lorencillo-baby landed on Isla with his beautiful cache of gold." Jessica jiggled her eyebrows in a comical Groucho Marx imitation. "Maybe we should be looking at that empty piece of land at Sac Bajo where the water is shallow and calmer. Nice sandy area, good for anchoring a boat."

Yasmin pulled her admiring gaze away from the glossy *Italika*. "Sure, any excuse to drive my new toy."

Inside the house, Yasmin quickly pulled on a long-sleeved t-shirt and liberally applied insect repellant to her bare legs, hands and neck. "The mosquitoes will be brutal there." When finished she passed the can to Jessica, then picked two bottles of water out of her fridge, and her keys from the kitchen counter.

"My favorite tropical perfume, *Deep Woods Off*," Jessica said, spraying any bit of exposed skin. She added enthusiastically, "Let's hit the road. We've got a treasure to find."

Chapter 12

November 8th Early afternoon

Zipping along on the motorcycle, Yasmin slowed frequently for the numerous *topes*, speed bumps. *Topes* were a way of life in Mexico, made from concrete, or humped asphalt, or thick lengths of rope laid across the road. Some were marked with warning signs; others were painted with reflective yellow paint that wore off with the repeated thumping of tires. A few were neither painted nor marked, you just had to know where they were. If she didn't pay attention, the abrupt changes to the road surface were capable of upsetting the bike, spilling both her and Jessica onto the hard asphalt surface.

When they reached the end of the public road, Yasmin stopped and stared at the muddy road. She sighed, and reluctantly steered her new moto onto the sandy road that led east through the swampy low-lying area of Sac Bajo. The entire area was covered in sand, clay, and the decomposing shells of millions of dead mollusks that had expired over the centuries, and surrounded by mangroves, a protected bush that grew in salty areas. The road was potholed and slippery with sea water seepage. Hardly anyone came to this part of the island, usually only a few late-night party animals parking in the bushes and consuming cases of *Tecate* or *Dos XX* cervezas. The thick undergrowth was littered with discarded beer bottles, liquor bottles, and food wrappers.

"Damn, this is slippery." Yasmin swore softly as she swerved to avoid a large mud puddle. "My poor new moto, it's going to be filthy."

"No kidding," Jessica agreed, clutching Yasmin as the back wheel on the motor-scooter slipped in the mud. "Jesus, don't dump us in that goop. It's probably full of bird poop and bacteria."

"People pay good money to roll in the mud at the flamingo reserve," Yasmin said with a giggle in her voice, as she gunned the engine, spraying muck into the air.

"Seriously? What is wrong with them?"

"It's supposed to be good for your skin." Yasmin turned to smile at Jessica and then noticed out of the corner of her eye a large branch was hanging over the trail, about to knock her in the head. "Whoa! Duck Jessica."

"That was close." Jessica muttered, "So bathing in mud, seriously?"

"Si, it's a big deal for tourists to take a boat ride from Rio Lagartos to where the birds nest, roll in the mud, and ride back to the town with the white goop drying on their skin."

"Holy hell, they must stink."

"Yes, they do."

Jessica pointed left. "Looks like we have to turn here, everything else is under water."

Yasmin turned down another overgrown pathway, noticing a large metal gate blocking the road. She said, "Someone has made a pathway around the gate, we can sneak past."

As they reached the end of the road, the sandy beach and calm turquoise water peaked through the thick cluster of mangrove trees. The women parked the motor-scooter and pulled off the hot helmets. Jessica finger-combed her hair, trying unsuccessfully to fluff up the sweat dampened strands. "Whew, hot. I'll never get used to the humidity."

"No, you probably won't," Yasmin grimaced as she slapped at a mosquito biting her cheek, "I've lived on Isla all my life, and I still suffer on days like this."

Turning slowly around, Jessica surveyed the area, "So, now what? Where should we look?"

Yasmin walked to the edge of the water and looked out at the various sail boats anchored in the bay. "This is a good spot for a ship to drop anchor, that's for sure. But things could have changed over the centuries. Lorencillo de Graaf raided Veracruz and then sailed to Isla with his booty in, what did you tell me, 1683? That's more than three hundred years ago."

"Are you trying to depress me?" Jessica tilted her head to the side, her face scrunched in a frown. "If you are, you are succeeding."

Pulling her phone from her pocket, Yasmin flicked to the photo that Jessica had taken of what they assumed was a map. It still didn't make any sense. It could be a crude topographical outline, but the lines just didn't match up to anything that they had seen so far. "I don't know. Let's just hike around on this flat area, anywhere that isn't under water. This is beginning to feel like a hopeless quest."

Two hours later, Jessica yelled, "Enough!" She was hot and cranky, and done—so done—with the mosquitoes. "Let's go."

Swiping at the sweat on her face, Yasmin nodded. "Yeah, I'm thirsty and hungry, and I need a shower and clean clothes. Let's get going."

As Yasmin slowly negotiated her motor scooter back through the slippery and narrow roadway, she suddenly pulled back on the throttle, whispering, "Jessica, is that a person skulking in the bushes?"

"Where?"

"Over there. I saw a flash of movement." Stopping, Yasmin put her feet down on either side of the motor-scooter to balance it, pointing at a bush that jiggled slightly in the muggy afternoon heat.

Scrutinizing the undergrowth where Yasmin was pointing, Jessica said, "I'm not sure, but I think I see a dog." She slid off the back seat, walking quietly towards the shrub. Squatting down she saw two brown eyes peering anxiously at her. "Here boy, come here. We won't hurt you," she softly coaxed.

"We don't have a lot of time, Jessica, we really have to get going."

Jessica kept looking towards the dog, but not making direct eye contact. "Just give me a minute or two," she said, maintaining a calm tone in her voice. "Come on little fella, let's have a look at you." The brown and grey scruffy mutt timidly belly-crawled towards Jessica. "Come on baby, just a little further." Trembling, the dog edged close enough that she could reach out and gently ease him into her arms. "Poor baby, you're bone-thin and filthy, and covered with big fat ticks."

"Then leave him! I don't want him near me."

"Nope. Not leaving him," Jessica retorted, ignoring Yasmin's discomfort. She was well aware that in Yasmin's family, dogs were a roof-top alarm system, not pets. Yasmin's mother would have pitched an almighty hissy fit if one of her children had brought a pet into the house.

Yasmin frowned at Jessica, her displeasure sizzling in her expression.

"Don't worry, I'll take him to my place." Jessica smiled down at the dog as she hoisted herself onto the back seat. "You'll love my place, sweetie. I know you will."

Twisting to glare over her shoulder at Jessica and the scruffy mutt, Yasmin said, "Hang on."

Straddling the back of the *moto* with the trembling dog clutched securely in her arms, Jessica said, "Hey girl, take it easy on those *topes*. Otherwise, the mutt and I are going to end up on our collective asses in the middle of the road." The pooch really was grubby. No time to properly clean him up before going to work, but at least she could give him water, a safe place to sleep and a good meal. *A good meal. Really? What exactly did she have in her fridge that a dog could eat? Condiments? Wine? Okay, problema número uno. Food.*

"Yassy, can you stop at our neighborhood *tienda*?"

"Why?" Concentrating on the road ahead, Yasmin sounded puzzled at Jessica's request. "Do you want some fruit? Or veggies?"

"Dog food. I need to buy the mutt some food."

Yasmin huffed, annoyed. "Great. So, when we are both late for work, I can tell Carlos it was your fault this time?"

"Sure, sure. No worries. You'll have to be quick though."

"Me. What are you talking about? I'm not buying the food for it." Yasmin swerved a little as she turned to scowl at Jessica.

"Oh, okay. You can hold the dog, and I'll run into the store." Jessica suppressed a wicked grin, her blue eyes snapping with mischief.

"Damn it, Jessica!" A few minutes later Yasmin stopped her mud-caked moto in front of a tiny corner store. "Do you have money? Or am I also paying for the food?"

"I have money, back at the house. So, yeah, you are paying for the food. I'll pay you back when I get to work."

"Fine." Yasmin tossed her hands, palms up, into the air. "What do I get?"

"A couple of cans of dog food, and a small sack of the dry stuff. Any kind will do for now. I'll get him better food tomorrow."

Waiting outside the store, Jessica let her eyes roam over the vibrant jumble partially blocking the entrance. Wooden crates containing yellow mangoes, deep green jalapeño peppers, red tomatoes, orange papayas, and green limes were stacked on the concrete steps. Mesh sacks containing smooth white onions, fat orange carrots, or pale green cabbages leaned against the walls. A rainbow assortment of inexpensive brooms with their colorful heads turned upwards were displayed in a blue plastic barrel. A bright red awning advertising *Coca-Cola* partially shaded the gloomy interior from the afternoon sun. Inside the store were floor to ceiling shelves, stuffed with bottles of cleaning liquids and oils. Dried chili peppers, spices, and ingredients for *mole* sauce added to the sensory confusion. It was nothing like any corner store she had seen in Canada. Owned by a close-knit island family, the store was one of Jessica's favorite places to buy freshly squeezed orange juice and ripe mangoes for breakfast.

Ten minutes later Yasmin irritably shoved a bag at Jessica, "Here, but the milk is mine for coffee tomorrow morning," she said, and hopped on the scooter. Jessica grinned at Yasmin's back, resisting a snappy comeback. She hung onto the dog and the dog food, tightly clamping her knees and thigh muscles to the scooter. Just like the locals, she thought, the ladies who can clutch two toddlers and ride behind their husbands without falling ass-over-teakettle off the back.

Back at her little house, Jessica slid off the motor scooter and thanked Yasmin for the ride home and the dog food. "See you later at work. I have to find a spot where I can secure this little guy until I get a chance to wash him and pull off the ticks."

"Yeah, well have fun with that. I have to wash the mud off my motorbike and then have my own shower." Yasmin flapped her hand in a dismissive wave, "I'll see you at work," she said as she drove off, obviously miffed at Jessica for dragging the dog home on her new, but considerably less shiny *Italika*.

"Don't worry, little buddy. She'll get over it in a few minutes. She doesn't stay unhappy for very long," Jessica said as she dropped the bag of pet food on her front steps. Then, juggling the dog and her keys and phone, she awkwardly unlocked her front door.

"Welcome to your new home," she said as she walked the short distance through the house and opened the back door leading to the fenced yard. "You can do your business out here, while I get ready for work."

A short time later, when Jessica had showered and changed into fresh clothes for work, she showed the as-yet-unnamed dog the tiny spare room that doubled as a storage area, or occasionally a cramped guest room. "Okay, dude. Here's how this works. I go to work. You stay in here." Giving him a blanket, a water bowl and a dish of food, she added, "I'll be back later, and will take you for a pee-poop walk. Then we come back, and you go to sleep. As do I. Tomorrow we'll figure out a better arrangement for you."

She looked at the pooch, shaking her head. *What the hell have I done? A dog. A furry complication.*

Chapter 13

November 8th Mid-night

"Yasmin!" Carlos called out, stopping Jessica and Yasmin just as they were about to exit the *Loco Lobo* through the employees-only security gate. Yasmin was digging in her large navy-blue purse for something. *Probably searching for the keys for her new moto*, he thought. "I know tomorrow is your day off, but would you and Jessica like to go on a sunset cruise around the island tomorrow evening? Ramon Poot has a forty-two-footer, and he has offered to take us out for drinks and snacks." Carlos smiled, mentally crossing his fingers that she would say yes. *Please say yes.*

Yasmin glanced hopefully towards Jessica, who nodded. "Sure, that'd be great, Carlos. We haven't done anything fun for ages. What time? And where?"

"Six-thirty at the wharf behind the gas station, the other side of the *Bally Hoo Restaurante*."

"Sounds good, thank you." Yasmin waved goodnight. "See you there."

"Night Carlos," Jessica added, "thanks for the invite."

"You're welcome, see you tomorrow," he replied. Ensuring the two women were part way down the street and out of sight, he spun back towards his office with a little two-step happy-dance. Then he heard a light chuckle behind him. He turned his head in time to see Isabella, his assistant bartender, laughing as she left the restaurant. Carlos shrugged, *Oh well*, as his dad was fond of saying, *there's no fool like an old fool, especially when it comes to pretty women.* He segued into his nightly shutdown routine, checking the roll-down security doors and turning off the overhead lights. There wasn't an alarm system to set, because there weren't any monitoring companies on the island. He had good security for the restaurant, but he also relied on people knowing who he was and being smart enough not to steal from him. He locked the staff gate behind himself, giving it a hard pull to double-check the lock was secure. Tomorrow was another day.

Chapter 14

November 9th Sunset

An hour before sundown on the following day, the cruiser *Mi Bonita Estella* slipped away from the wharf near the *Bally Hoo Restaurante*, with a group of twelve on board. Carlos felt a little poke of jealousy watching Ramon confidently maneuver the big yacht through the palm shrouded Makax Lagoon towards the open ocean.

The light salty breeze cooled his skin while the sun-warmed deck was soothing to his bare feet. He shifted his weight in sync to the gentle motion of the yacht as it slid through the calm turquoise water. Boats were his passion. He didn't own one, yet, but it was on his bucket list. Luckily, he had a few friends who owned cruisers. Carrying two open bottles of wine, he slowly made his way forward, chatting with friends and topping off their glasses. His target was the bow where Yasmin sat relaxed in a cross-legged position on the deck. She looked fabulous—long and lean, dark curly hair with lighter almost caramel-colored highlights, white sunglasses, white shorts, and a dark blue top. She belonged on a boat. On his boat.

"Yasmin? *Tinto o blanco*?" he offered, holding up first one bottle of wine, then the other.

She peered over the top of her sunglasses, making contact with Carlos' deep brown eyes, "Tinto, por favor."

"Good choice." He tilted a generous amount of red wine into her glass. "Your favorite, I think, Salentein Malbec from Argentina."

"How did you know this is my favorite?"

"I confess," he said, grinning like a little kid caught in a small fib, "I asked Jessica."

"Thank you, I appreciate your thoughtfulness."

"De nada. Did you do anything interesting this morning?"

"Not unless you count grocery shopping, laundry and household chores as interesting."

"Er, no," he said, laughing as he shook his head, "not very interesting to me." He was reluctant to admit to Yasmin he had a housekeeper who looked after him and his *casa*. In both of their families the mothers and any female children typically shared the housework. The teenage sons were usually pampered by their mothers until a wife took over the care and feeding of the son. The husbands worked; they didn't do chores. But with the influx of foreigners into Mexico, many of Yasmin's generation had begun to hope that their boyfriends and husbands might actually help with household tasks—or not, as it frequently turned out.

His housekeeper, Luz, had her own key and she came and went as it suited her and her family's schedule. She and her brood joined in with the large boisterous Mendoza clan for celebrations of weddings, birthdays, baptisms, and the important fifteenth birthday for females, their *quince años*. Once a week Luz arrived to clean, do the laundry, and bring the basics of coffee, fresh fruit, milk, sugar, and breakfast makings. Most of his meals were eaten at the restaurant, with the exception of that important first cup of morning coffee. His poor, and in her mind deprived, mother was impatiently waiting for him to settle down and provide her with more grandchildren, like his younger siblings had so obligingly produced. His mother frequently reminded him; he was still *Tio* Carlos, an uncle, not a *papi*.

"I'm sorry, Yasmin, I was thinking about work. What did you just say?"

Yasmin repeated the question, "I just asked, where are we headed?"

"South through the Makax Lagoon, past the new mansion on the point, and then along to

Garrafon Park, around the point at Punta Sur, and along the eastern side back to Playa Norte. Okay?"

"Yes, perfect. Just curious." She glanced away, "Do you know much about the island geography?"

He paused, considering the question. First she was interested in laws about buried treasure, now about the geography of the island. It must be for the 'novel' that she was writing. "Yes, a little. Like you, I have lived here most of my life. What do you want to know?"

"Do you think the land area at the end of Sac Bajo, the part that is between Laguna Makax and the ocean, has increased over the years?" She pointed at the shoreline.

"Probably. Why?"

"I was just wondering if it was bigger now than say a few hundred years ago. Perhaps the mangrove trees have helped create a base for more land to form." She faltered, adding in a whisper, "It's background information for my novel of course, but I don't want anyone to know that I am writing a book until it's finished."

Carlos nodded seriously, as if he believed her lie. "Of course, of course." He mimed zipping his lips shut. "I will say nothing. I'll ask Ramon to give us a better look at that area."

Leaving Yasmin to enjoy the view, Carlos wandered back to the cockpit where Ramon was steering his cruiser. "Hey, *pendejo*." He bumped fists with his friend. "Can we get a little closer to that area over there?" He indicated the sand spit on his left.

"It's pretty shallow, but yeah, I can get a bit closer. Why?" Ramon's eyes continuously scanned the water, depth sounder and shoreline looking for problems. Carlos had been on Ramon's boat before and knew the hull didn't draw much water in depth, but the ocean floor shifted continuously with wind and wave action.

"Just curious. I used to hang around that area on Saturday nights drinking with the guys. Just wondering if it still looks the same."

Ramon snorted, "Yep, probably, at least it did when I spent my Saturday nights drinking with my buddies, ten years after you did—old man."

"Shut the hell up, I'm only thirty-nine." Carlos puffed out his chest while playfully cocking one arm in a muscle-builder pose. "See?" he quipped through taut lips as he tightly cramped his stomach muscles against his ribs. "I'm in my prime."

"Uh huh, sure you are." Ramon slowly swung the wheel over and pointed the cruiser slightly south, pulling closer to the shoreline. "I saw you making eyes at the young talent over there." He indicated in Yasmin's direction with his chin, chuckling. "Old man."

As the yacht slid closer to the land, Carlos watched Yasmin stand and move closer to the bow. He studied her expression as she gripped the bow rail. She appeared to be staring intently at the hilly area behind the Hacienda Mundaca.

"Jessica, hey Jessica." Carlos heard Yasmin call, waving her arm overhead.

Turning away from a three-way conversation, Jessica replied, "What?"

Beckoning with her hand, Yasmin said, "Come here, I want to show you something."

"Just a minute," Jessica answered, turning to excuse herself from the group before she carefully made her way towards Yasmin. "What's so important?"

Attentive to the byplay between the two women, Carlos watched as Yasmin pointed towards the center of the island. She seemed to be whispering to Jessica. He could see her lips moving but couldn't hear what was being said. Intrigued, he watched as Jessica clenched her fists straight down by her sides, holding back her natural exuberance, not the Jessica he knew. She was normally very animated. *What the hell are they up to?*

Chapter 15

November 10th Late morning

Jessica chuckled at the irony of their situation. Just yesterday they had spent a relaxing evening on Ramon's yacht. Today they were once again dragging their butts through the mosquito-infested jungle at the Hacienda Mundaca Park, searching for the elusive buried treasure.

She hated the buzzing, biting, blood-thirsty mosquitoes. She hated her sweat-soaked top, clinging to her body. She really hated not finding anything—again. They were so sure this time. The line of the hills, well, not really hills, but higher knobs on an otherwise nearly flat island seemed to match the fading scrawls of what they thought was a map. Staring at a semi-collapsed cave, an area carved out of the limestone by centuries of rainwater, she was sure it had to be the right place. As she scuffed the toe of her sandal in the dirt, her eyes caught a glint of dull metal. Bending down, she carefully cleared away the leaves, and pulled an irregular-shaped object from the earth. Scratching it lightly with a fingernail, Jessica could see it was made of gold. *Holy crap.*

"Hey, Yasmin! Over here!" Jessica yelled.

Yasmin plodded over to where Jessica was standing. "What?" she asked, wiping a piece of paper towel across her forehead in an attempt to mop up the sweat relentlessly sliding towards her eyes.

"This." Jessica held a not-quite-round piece of metal between her thumb and finger, "I think it's a Spanish coin."

"Oh my God, seriously? A Spanish coin? Really?"

"Now you're too loud," Jessica teased. "Keep it down. But yeah, look at the markings on it. One side has this straight cross, and the other side has a bunch of carvings with the number eight at the top." She pointed at the number stamped in the metal. "I did a little online research while I fueled up with my morning coffee. I'm pretty sure this is a Spanish doubloon, or eight escudos."

"Wait, did you only find one coin?" Yasmin's sweat-streaked face was etched with disappointment.

"Yep, but I figure where there is one, there will be more of these little beauties. Come on, let's search this area." Jessica bent closer to the earth, carefully sweeping aside rotting vegetation as she peered under plants.

Plunking herself down on a nearby rock, Yasmin puffed air up towards her wet bangs, attempting to blow them away from her eyes. "Why don't we just rent a metal detector? It would be a lot easier."

"Yeah? And how's that going to play out?" Jessica's eyebrows flicked up, as she spoke with a breathless, southern-belle lilt to her voice. "Why we just thought we would roam through this *real purdy* jungle looking for jewelry that tourists might have lost. We all just thought it would be so much fun to do."

"Well, there has to be a better way than searching on our hands and knees. Maybe that scruffy mutt you dragged home can help us," Yasmin grumbled.

"I don't think dogs can track metal. Clothes, people, cadavers, food, things that have a distinct smell, but metal, I don't think that's possible." Jessica sniffed the coin, thinking.

"Humph. So he's useless. That's what you should name him, Useless. The only thing he's good for is eating, pooping, and sleeping."

Jessica did an eye-roll. Yasmin's normally cheerful attitude had resurfaced yesterday while they were on Ramon's boat, but today was again buried as deeply as the treasure they were hunting. Probably, Jessica assumed, caused by the frustration of the search, along with the humidity, heat and hungry mosquitoes.

"Nope," Jessica said, "his name is Sparky, or *Chispita* in Spanish. He reminds me of that little terrier in the John Travolta movie, the one about the fallen angel *Michael*."

Yasmin retorted, "I still think Useless is a better name." She slowly got to her feet, tugging at her sweat-soaked t-shirt, prying the wet material away from her hot skin.

"He's a good boy. He hasn't had any accidents in the house, and he doesn't sleep on my furniture." Jessica smiled as she thought about what a dirty skinny mess he was when she found him just two days ago at Sac Bajo. "He's had a bath and been treated for fleas and ticks. A few more weeks of good food and he'll be a handsome little dude."

"Whatever." Yasmin flapped her hand dismissively. "I still think we need a metal detector."

"I'm not sure we can rent one. We might have to buy one, in Cancun. And then how the heck do we hide it?" Jessica gratefully stretched her back muscles as she straightened up from searching the ground. "All we have for transport is your moto, or taxis. Either way people will wonder what we are up to."

"Look, I know it's only two, and we don't have to be at work until four, but I can't do anymore of this searching today. Everything hurts from bending and searching. The mosquitos have drained a few liters of my blood, and I need food. Let's go." Yasmin pleaded.

Twenty minutes later, Jessica hopped off Yasmin's moto in front of her little house in the colonias. "Okay see you in a couple of hours." She waved goodbye as she unlocked her front door. "Thanks for the ride."

The place that she rented in La Gloria made Jessica smile every time she arrived home. The local owners had painted it a cheery Caribbean combination of hues, with orange walls, pink window frames, and a glossy turquoise door. Inside was more of the same wild combination of colors. She had added a comfortable chair and a two-seater navy blue sofa, with a stack of turquoise, orange, yellow, and pink throw cushions. Her wacky little slice of paradise.

Sharing an enthusiastic greeting with Sparky, Jessica held open the back door, giving him access to her tiny yard. "Do your business. Pees and poops. *Rápido, rápido.*" The short-legged, terrier-cross mutt searched the yard with focused concentration, hunting for clues as to birds, cats, dogs, or humans that had crossed into his territory. He was more interested in what his nose could tell him than he was in relieving himself. Leaning on the frame of the door, Jessica watched his intense search of the tiny yard. *Could a dog smell metal? Sparky certainly had a nose for smells.* It would be worth doing a Google search on the internet, just out of curiosity. Leave no stone unturned, and all that.

Chapter 16

November 10ᵗʰ Afternoon

Pushing aside a partially eaten tomato, lettuce and cheese sandwich, Jessica rested her elbows on her turquoise-painted wooden kitchen table. She flicked the screen on her smartphone, searching for information on the worth of the gold doubloons. As it turned out the coin she had found was an *escudo* because it was made of gold. The silver doubloons were called *reales*.

Glancing over at Sparky, Jessica smiled, "Interesting information, hey bud? But show me the money!" He thumped his tail enthusiastically, happy to be included in the conversation.

Jessica continued scanning pages and searching for more information about the doubloons. The internet listed many variables for the value of the coin. At .218 of a Troy ounce, the coin's worth fluctuated with the current price of gold, so around four hundred American dollars at today's value. However, as pirate treasure, with a long and fascinating history — it could be worth from four thousand to tens of thousands of American dollars per coin, according to the web.

"Well damn, one coin and we're already rich." She gleefully scratched Sparky's head. "Yasmin will be so impressed. Now all we have to do is figure out a way to cash this thing in without ending up in prison. Going to prison is definitely not on my list of things to do before I die." Sometimes her dark sense of humor confused her friends, thinking her callous and unfeeling. Not true. Just realistic. Growing up in a big city with a dad and two older brothers who were all firefighters, she had seen and heard about a lot of nasty, unpleasant things. Add to that her mother's nursing career, and conversations around the dinner table could get a bit graphic at times.

Thinking about her close-knit family, she realized that she probably wouldn't be able to recount this little adventure at a clan dinner, being as what she and Yasmin were doing was not exactly legal in Mexico—okay, not legal at all. Her parents and siblings would probably not be thrilled with her exploits. In many other countries of the world, if she and Yasmin did find the stash, the authorities would normally claim the treasure for the federal government and then award them a ten percent finder's fee. But, according to the *notario* that Yasmin consulted, no such luck in Mexico. Oh well, just roll with the punches, and keep on smiling.

"Okay, now, let's see what we can find out about sniffer dogs." Poking the small keys, she typed 'tracking dogs' in the search parameter.

Rapidly reading various websites, she quickly became engrossed in the information. Besides the historical practice of using dogs for hunting wildlife and birds, sniffer dogs could be trained to search for lost people, cadavers, illegal drugs, and explosives. There were even specially trained detection dogs that could search out contraband mobile phones in prisons, and stashes of currency in drug houses. Dogs had, on average, about one hundred fifty to two hundred million scent receptors in their noses, while humans were an underprivileged species with only five million receptors. *Maybe, just maybe, Yasmin was onto something. Maybe Sparky could sniff out the buried treasure. How cool would that be?*

Flicking through a few more pages on the internet, Jessica noticed a webpage about ore-sniffing dogs. Now that's really interesting, specially trained dogs that could sniff out gold deposits. But could she train a Mexican street dog to do the same job as these bazillion-dollar dogs from Europe?

"Hey, Sparky. You want to learn a new game?" Jessica turned to look at the mutt. He waved his short feathery tail. Yep, he was ready for some fun. His quizzical brown eyes watched her. Yasmin had agreed that Jessica would hang on to the coin until they decided what to do with it. It was tucked into her small laptop-sized safe, one that she had installed just in case someone broke into her home looking for electronics to steal and sell. She opened the safe and carefully unwrapped the gold coin, thinking how ironic it was to treat it so gently considering it had spent the last few hundred years buried in the ground.

"Come on, boy, let's play for a few minutes." Jessica scooped up a handful of doggie kibble, stuffing them in the pocket of her shorts. "Okay, easy stuff first." She held the coin under the dog's nose, watching as he sniffed then looked at her with questioning eyes. *Okay, that's not food, so now what?* He seemed to be asking.

Jessica gave him a piece of kibble. "Good boy, good boy, Sparky." Walking over to her couch, she tucked the coin under one of the throw pillows. "Okay, find it!" Jessica exclaimed excitedly, pointing at the pillow. "Search."

Confused, the pooch sat down, his tail swishing back and forth as his eyes searched her face for a clue.

Next Jessica tucked a couple of pieces of dog kibble under the pillow. "Search. Find." She said.

Sparky willingly hopped up on the couch and stuck his nose under the pillow. He gobbled up the small treat and hopped back down to the floor, waiting to see what happened next.

"Well that didn't work out quite the way I had planned." Jessica tilted her head to one side, "Okay, let's try again. Since you are a Mexican mutt, maybe I should speak Spanish to you instead of English." Picking up her phone, she quickly thumbed 'find' into the Google translation app. "*Buscar*. Okay, let's try this again." Jessica picked up the doubloon and let the dog sniff it again. Then she hid it under the pillow along with two pieces of kibble. "*Buscar. Buscar.*"

The dog leapt on the couch and poked his nose under the pillow, until he could reach the treats. One gulp and the snack was gone. He looked at Jessica, and wagged his tail.

"Yeah, yeah, good boy," she responded with mild enthusiasm. Well, this wasn't exactly working to plan. "Okay, let's try one more time, just in case you get the idea." Repeating the routine of letting the dog smell the coin, then placing it under the pillow with a couple of treats, Jessica again gave him the command. "*Buscar.*"

Again he hopped up on the couch and stuck his nose under the cushion. This time his nose accidentally pushed the coin out along with the treats. "Yes! Awesome job, Sparky," Jessica exclaimed, patting his head and rubbing his ears. "Great job." His tail flashed back and forth rapidly in agreement, his keen brown eyes shining with excitement.

"Ya done good." Jessica hugged the thin little mutt. "I have to get ready for work now. We'll try again tomorrow."

Chapter 17

November 10th Late afternoon

Yasmin parked her shiny *Italika* motor-scooter among a long line of other motos. It was a parking area commonly used by workers who staffed the numerous restaurants and bars along Hidalgo Avenue. She pulled off her helmet and shook out her dark, shoulder-length hair. Stupid helmet. It was unflattering, and crushed her hair. Fortunately, her natural curls rapidly bounced back in the humid tropical afternoon.

Slinging her bag over her shoulder, she strode along the street headed to the *Loco Lobo*, for yet another busy eight or nine hours. What a frustrating week this had been. Work. Sleep. Eat. And in her free time, tramp through the hot jungle searching for what was probably nothing more than a legend. One more week, and that was it. She wasn't going to let the fantasy of buried treasure control her life. She had things to do. Places to see. *And fingers-crossed, maybe something will develop between*

Carlos and me. Just thinking of Carlos brought goosebumps to her arms.

Her mother was pushing hard for Yasmin to settle down, get married, and produce grandbabies. She considered an unmarried twenty-eight-year-old Latina woman as a borderline hopeless case. According to her, Yasmin should have been married and producing babies as soon as she graduated from college at the ripe old age of eighteen. Uff. Now that would have been a really boring life.

It was fortunate that her parents had decided to move to Mérida, a larger city in the Yucatan peninsula. Thankfully, her mother had wanted to be closer to her older daughter Adriana with her two sweet little boys, six-year-old Eduard and eight-year-old Enrique. Her mom also liked being closer to the upscale stores, gourmet restaurants, and live theatre performances. Yasmin was relishing her new-found freedom, far away from her mother's match-making attempts. Her *papi*, her daddy, was her rock. He had encouraged her to learn English at a very early age. Being fluent in more than one language gave her an edge for getting a good paying job in a resort community like Isla Mujeres. Smiling at the memory of her *papi* arguing with her mom, insisting Yasmin should watch television cartoons on the English-only channels. A funny way to learn another language, but such a simple way to absorb the colloquialisms and expressions.

Jessica, on the other hand, was so much luckier, Yasmin thought. When she wanted a colorful full-sleeve tattoo with flowers and turtles and sea creatures, she went ahead and got one. If she wanted to decorate both ears with a collection of earrings, she did that as well. Her family didn't have any expectations of what their strong-willed daughter would do with her life. Just be happy. One evening, after a few margaritas, Jessica had spoken emotionally about her parents' unconditional love and their philosophy of life: Be happy, and be a good person. Well, she was both of those things, Yasmin thought, happy and nice. Okay, maybe her friend did sample a variety of men. She really enjoyed sex. In Jessica's mind it was simply a great way to get some cardio exercise, to feel invigorated and relaxed.

In Yasmin's culture, young women were taught that sex was to produce babies and not for fun. Sometimes being a Latina woman was such a pain in the butt. She was expected to look sexy, with long hair, lots of cleavage, full makeup, dangling earrings, tight clothes, and stiletto heels. But she was expected to act modest, demure, and self-effacing around men. Talk about a mixed message. Jeez. As for getting a tattoo, never going to happen. When she was only nine years old, she had promised her father that she would never, ever deface her body with a tattoo of any kind. She would never break a promise to her beloved *papi*.

"Hey, amiga, why the scowl on your face?" Jessica teased as she noticed Yasmin entering the bar from the street patio.

"What?" Yasmin purposely dithered, not wanting to openly admit she was envious of Jessica's freedom. "Oh, hi Jessica, I was just thinking about our recent project, you know, our hobby." Yasmin spoke in code, afraid to actually say the words *treasure hunting* out loud. "Just feeling annoyed that we haven't made a lot of progress." Whispering quietly, they slowly walked towards the staff area.

Jessica murmured, "I don't know about that, I think we have made great progress. Finding that little trinket and all," she winked.

"Yeah, I guess you're right, but still, what if we can't keep it? It's a bit frustrating." Yasmin glanced around. No one appeared to be listening to their conversation.

"Well, I have a little surprise for you..." Jessica was grinning at Yasmin with a smile that said *come on, ask me, ask me, I can't wait to tell you.*

"Really?" Yasmin conspiratorially leaned towards Jessica, "What's your big secret?"

Jessica bent in close to her ear, speaking softly, "I researched the coin. It could be worth anywhere from four hundred dollars to ten thousand dollars depending on how we sell it."

"What. No. You're kidding me." She stifled a yell, remembering that they were at work. "That much?"

"Yes. And that's not all. I think I can teach Sparky to sniff out gold."

"Seriously?" Yasmin's deep green eyes rounded in surprise. "I was only joking about that."

"Yes, seriously. I researched ore-sniffing dogs on the internet. It's possible. I think the little dude is part terrier, which gives him a great sniffing nose. Plus, he seems pretty darn smart."

Still skeptical, Yasmin pulled her head back to stare directly at Jessica's Nordic-blue eyes, "Are you BS-ing me?"

"Nope. Cross my heart and hope to die, I am telling you the truth," she said, sketching a cross over her heart with a finger. "I know it takes months or years to train scent dogs, but Sparky has an amazing nose. I really think I can teach him to find gold. We practiced a bit earlier this afternoon, and he caught on really quick." Jessica glanced towards the street-side patio and caught a glimpse of two men headed towards them. "Damn it, Kirk and Ryan are here," she muttered a warning to Yasmin. "Be careful of what you say."

Yasmin turned and quickly plastered a fake happy-server smile on her face. "Good afternoon guys. What can we get you?" Ryan, she noticed, was grinning at Jessica. He apparently had recovered from her casual rejection of him a few days ago. But Kirk seemed to have a perpetual scowl on his face, like a bratty, spoiled little boy. With dark hair, blue eyes, and a chiseled jaw, he was a good-looking guy, but something about him made her particularly uneasy.

Ryan winked at Yasmin. "Two cervezas," he said.

"Sure, coming right up." Yasmin reached into the cooler and pulled out two Sol beers. "I haven't signed in yet for my shift, so I'll let Isabella ring up the order for you." She slid the two bottles onto the countertop, turning away to stash her bag in the staff area.

Kirk swiftly reached out and tightly gripped her upper arm, "Hey! Can't you at least say hello?"

Yasmin pointedly looked at his hand, then stared at him, waiting for him to get the message to remove it.

Glowering, he mumbled, "Whatever," and dropped his hand. "You are always in a big hurry, no time to be friendly."

She coolly regarded him, "I'm sorry, but I have to put my things away." She went into the tiny staff area, closed the door, and leaned back against it. *That guy truly gives me the willies.*

Chapter 18

November 10th Late evening

Six beers later, Kirk was fed up with trying to chat up Yasmin. He tossed enough money on the table to cover their tab, but nothing for a tip.

"Come on, let's go. Someplace where the company is more pleasant." Kirk forcefully shoved back his chair. The back legs caught momentarily on the uneven floor surface and overbalanced. The crash of the wooden chair striking the hard floor reverberated through the busy restaurant, causing several people to glance up.

Ryan reached over and lightly tapped Kirk's forearm. "Jesus, man, calm down. Don't be such a jerk."

Kirk furiously knocked away his hand. "I said, let's go." Seething, he stomped out of the bar. That bitch had no idea who she was messing with. He didn't need to ask her permission to touch her. He would take what he wanted when the time and place was right. It was all about timing. He knew he shouldn't have created a scene back at the *Loco Lobo*, but his lightning-quick temper had flared up before he could smother it. It might be time to leave the island for a more welcoming place, someplace where he could easily satisfy his taste in women and no one would notice, or if they did notice, they wouldn't care one damn bit.

Angrily storming past the abandoned entrance of a defunct late-night club, Kirk was outraged when he felt a strong arm wrap around his throat and squeeze hard, cutting off his air. He clawed at the arm, pulling with all his strength, kicking, aiming to stomp on the foot of his assailant. A steely voice hissed in his ear, "You will stay away from Yasmin if you wish to remain healthy, my friend. This is your only warning."

Kirk frantically tossed his head back in an attempt to head butt the other guy, to break his nose. His attacker dodged his head sideways out of the way. Unable to break loose, Kirk felt the pressure on his throat increase, cutting off his air until he slumped unconscious.

Inside the *Loco Lobo,* Ryan upended his beer and placed the bottle on the table. As he caught

Yasmin's questioning look, he shrugged his shoulders. *Sorry*, he mouthed. Out on the street he looked up and down Hidalgo Avenue but didn't see Kirk anywhere. By now he was probably quaffing back cold ones at another one of their favorite hangouts, *El Arrecife.* Ryan had a difficult time rolling his tongue around the double 'r' in the name, frequently using the English equivalent, *The Reef*, when hooking up with friends. Walking south on Hidalgo, Ryan glanced to his left at a crumbled pile of clothes in the entrance of a vacant night club. *Weird, not a normal place for a drunk to sleep off the booze, but hey, whatever, not my business.*

Closer to the square in Centro, *El Arrecife* was packed with young bodies, all talking and laughing at once, vying for attention from anyone of the opposite sex. Just another fun night in paradise, Ryan mused.

Squeezing past the throng, Ryan waved at the bartender, shouting. "Sol, por favor." He scanned the crowd, scrutinizing any tall dark-haired guy, but didn't see Kirk anywhere. That guy was seriously on a downer tonight so he could sulk by himself.

It's not like they were close long-term friends anyway, having recently met here on the island. Ryan didn't know much about Kirk's background other than he had lived for a time in Florida. Kirk was pretty darn close-mouthed about his life, side-stepping any questions about what he did for a living. Mostly he was just a chum to hang out with and to chase women. A drinking buddy. Ryan, on the other hand, had been unguarded, discussing his job in Minneapolis for a service contractor that installed underground pipes. Winters in the north were too cold for digging up streets, and he was able to get away for two to three months a year. It was a pretty sweet gig.

Ryan turned back to the bartender and signalled for another beer. Might as well enjoy himself. A few more weeks and he would have to return home to Minneapolis and a cold spring.

Hours later, after the late-night clubs had closed, the pile of clothes that Ryan had noticed earlier began to stir. Groaning, Kirk slowly eased himself into a sitting position. *What the hell had happened? I wasn't that drunk.*

Hanging onto the wall, Kirk pulled himself to his feet, gingerly testing his balance. His throat hurt like hell, and he winced in pain as he explored the area with his fingers. This didn't seem to be a robbery. He could feel that his gold chain with the attached shark's tooth still hung around his neck. His wallet and phone were both in his pockets. He recalled leaving the *Loco Lobo* headed towards *El Arrecife* and then he remembered the menace in the voice as a muscular arm clamped off his windpipe. Now he stank of cat piss, dog crap, and who knew what else. *Christ. What a damn mess.*

Whatever the guy had done to him, he had been out for at least a couple of hours. *He wants to play rough, well I can play rough too.* Kirk walked on unsteady legs towards the cheap local hotel where he had rented a room for two months. "Okay then, buddy. When I figure out who you are, next time we'll play by my rules."

Chapter 19

November 11th Late morning

"Sparky, we are going to play our special game again." Jessica affectionately grinned at the brown, and now much-whiter mutt. Even though he was clean and tick-free, Yasmin was still unhappy with the dog riding on her new moto, but she had finally agreed to include him in their search at the Hacienda Mundaca Park today.

The next challenge had been getting past the gatekeeper, Adela, with the dog. That had taken a bit of creative banter. Jessica had assured the woman that she was not going to abandon him in the park. She also promised she would pick up any doggie poop deposits. "See," she said, holding up the plastic container clipped on his leash that contained a roll of poop bags, "I'll clean up after him."

With a sarcastic smile, Adela gave Jessica one final warning, "Watch out for the crocodile," she said, quietly laughing. "He likes the taste of small dogs, especially well-fed small dogs. Last month he escaped and hot-footed it over to a nearby beach club, looking for tasty tourists. The police and city workers had to hogtie him and bring him back here." Her eyes crinkled in amusement as she struggled to keep a straight face. "He might still be hungry."

"Thank you for warning us," said Jessica, smiling thinly at the woman, thinking she was a bit too cheerful about that last statement. If it was true that the crocodile had been snacking on stray cats and dogs from the nearby colonia, that would be a horrific way for an animal to die.

They hiked back to where Jessica had scuffed up the Spanish coin with her foot. Carefully extracting the cloth wrapped doubloon from her front pocket, Jessica held the irregularly shaped coin under the dog's nose, thinking this was a long shot at best, but worth a try. "*Buscar*, Sparky, *buscar*." He looked at her quizzically, then bent his nose to the ground. He carefully scrutinized each square inch of ground, left and right, back and forth, up the hill and back down towards Jessica. Several minutes later he sat at her feet, wagging his feathery tail.

"Okay, well that didn't work out so well."

"Told ya." Yasmin sighed, "useless."

"How will we know, if we don't try?" Jessica snapped defensively. "Come on Sparky, let's try this again." She held the coin under his nose, repeating the command to *find it*. The dog pawed the dirt beside Jessica's foot, gave one sharp bark, and stared at her.

Puzzled, Jessica knelt down to examine the ground by Sparky's front feet. He barked again, once, pawing at the dirt. Jessica scratched with some difficulty in the hard-packed earth, burrowing to half a hand in depth before her fingers touched metal. "Oh my god, really?" Snatching up a small branch, she energetically stabbed the ground, dislodging two gold coins that matched the one in her pocket. "Yasmin, look!"

"*Dios mio!*" Yasmin exclaimed excitedly. "He did it. He found the treasure."

"Er, not exactly the whole treasure Yasmin." Jessica replied. "He's only found two, out of seventy-thousand. Maybe he just got lucky." Jessica carefully brushed the dirt from the two coins and handed one to Yasmin. "These are beautiful. So simple, and so old."

Reaching to take the coin, Yasmin's eyes glistened with emotion. "It's true. My grandmother's story about unrequited love and lost pirate treasure is true, it's not a fairy tale." Yasmin tightly clutched the gold doubloon in her hand, bouncing up and down, unable to contain her excitement. "Oh my god. Oh my god. Oh my god. It's true."

Sparky looked at Jessica, then yawned, and laid down on the pathway. He seemed to have lost interest in their new game. "Come on, boy, she quietly urged him, "don't give up now."

"No, no, Sparky, *buscar. Buscar.*" Yasmin reached down and anxiously tugged on his collar, urging him to find more coins. Instead he flipped over on his back, presenting his tummy for a scratch. "Sparky, find the gold!" Yasmin shouted in frustration, causing the dog to quickly roll onto his feet and scramble into the undergrowth.

"Shhh, Yasmin, we don't want to attract attention." Jessica made calming motions with her hands as she nervously glanced around. Fortunately, they had never seen anyone else during their three visits to the park. The facility seemed to be a well-kept secret, ignored by the thousands of daytime visitors who toured the island in rented golf carts. From what she had seen, there was only one retired man who maintained the gardens, and the attendant at the entrance gate. "Besides," Jessica added, "yelling just scares him. He won't search when he's frightened."

"Oh dear. I am so sorry, Sparky. I didn't mean to yell at you." Yasmin held her hand out, trying to coax him out from under the foliage. "Come here boy, I promise no more yelling."

Cautiously, Sparky stuck his nose out and allowed Yasmin to scratch his silky ears. Jessica reached down and picked him up, holding him in her arms and giving him a comforting hug. "It's okay, big boy, we are just a little stressed." She rummaged in another pocket and found a dog treat, "Here you go big boy, a reward for being so smart." Jessica cooed.

Setting the pooch down on the pathway, Jessica tried to interest him again in the gold coin. He simply laid down and looked at her, waiting. Trying not to show her frustration, Jessica picked up the small branch, playfully digging in the earth where she had found the coins. "Come on, boy. Let's play. *Buscar.*" Nothing. No reaction. "Well damn it. I guess that's it for today then." She slumped down on the ground, wondering what they should do next. This had seemed like the perfect solution—a treasure-sniffing mutt.

Abruptly, Sparky leapt up into a stiff-legged stance, his tail straight up from his back. A low growl rumbled through his chest, imitating the warning of a much larger dog.

"Sparky! What's wrong?" Jessica jumped to her feet, scanning around as she peered into the dense jungle. With one hand clutching Sparky's collar, she worried that he might take off after something, like the crocodile. And that would only end badly for Sparky.

Chapter 20

November 11th Mid-afternoon

Notario Luis Aguilar slid onto a bar stool at the *Loco Lobo*, bumping fists and slapping palms with Carlos in greeting. "Hey bud, haven't seen you for a few days. How's life?"

"Good, man. We're just coming into high season and I've been busy here at the bar." Reaching into the beer refrigerator, Carlos pulled out a cold Sol. He popped the cap with a practiced move, a quick flick using the spine of a large knife. "Come to collect that free cerveza I owe you?" He placed the beer in front of Luis then casually glanced around the bar to ensure everything was under control. Satisfied with what he saw, he turned his attention back to his friend.

"Cervezas, as in more than one, my friend, a lot more than one, for helping out your aspiring writer," Luis said, then chuckled lightly. "So where is the beautiful Miss Yasmin? And how is her award-winning novel coming along?"

Shrugging nonchalantly, Carlos played along with the story that Yasmin had told both him and Luis when she was looking for information on the laws governing treasure hunting in Mexico. "She doesn't work until later this afternoon. As for her progress on the novel, I don't have a clue. She's very close-mouthed about that. She said she didn't want too many people knowing in case she changed her mind and didn't write it." He shrugged again, "She doesn't want to be embarrassed if it doesn't happen."

Luis grinned and sipped his beer. "Okay, I get it. Hey, what happened to your arm?" He tilted his beer bottle towards Carlos' right forearm, indicating the deep scratch marks. "That looks serious."

"This?" Carlos casually moved his arm off the counter, rolling down both sleeves on his black linen shirt, covering the marks. "It's nothing, a little renovation project that went wrong. Just clumsy I guess." He popped the cap on a second beer and slid it towards his friend. "That one looks to be about finished."

"Thanks. Why don't you join me?" Luis asked. "After all, you are the owner of this joint."

"Ha, too early for me, I don't usually get out of here before midnight or later. If I start drinking beer now it will turn into a really long day." He grinned as he casually patted his hard, flat stomach muscles. "Besides, I'm trying to keep my weight down, and beer is a killer for me."

Suddenly quiet, Luis fiddled with the beer bottle, making a pattern on the bar top with circles of condensation. "I have a question to ask you."

"Yeah? What's up?"

"Have you noticed an American guy, tall, with dark hair and blue eyes, hanging around the island lately? Know the one I mean?"

"I know who you mean." Carlos nodded in agreement, keeping a neutral expression on his face. "Kirk something."

"I think I have seen him before, well, at least a photo of him." Luis stopped toying with his beer bottle and glanced at Carlos. "When I was visiting friends in Florida a couple of months ago, the cops were looking for a murder suspect that looked a hell of a lot like this dude. His face was splashed all over TV for the week that I was there."

Carlos locked his gaze on Luis. "What did he do?" Just the thought of a killer hanging around Yasmin spiked his heart rate. He could feel his blood thumping in his carotid artery.

"He's what they call a person-of-interest in a gruesome murder of a young Florida woman." Carlos watched as Luis set the beer bottle on the counter.

He seemed to relax a little now that he had voiced his concerns.

"How did she die?" Carlos asked. Breathing deep and steady, he willed his heart to slow down. Luis was not a rumor-monger. He had a lively intellect and a strong sense of honor. If he said he saw that Patterson guy on US television, then he undoubtedly did see him. Unless the guy had a doppelgänger, a twin.

"He drugged her with roofies, then raped her and cut her throat. Pretty damn gross." Luis stared at Carlos. "If this is the same guy, how did he get past airport security? He would've had to show a passport with his photo. Surely the airports would have been notified." Luis leaned back in the chair, a worried question in his eyes.

"That's no problem. There are lots of sport fishing boats that move back and forth between Florida and Mexico during the sailfish season. It's easy to hire on as a deck hand and hitch a ride. You just slip the captain a little extra cash. As soon as the yacht docks, you just leave your stuff and walk away before the harbor master boards to check documents." Pretending he was unconcerned about Luis' news, Carlos leaned his forearm on the countertop. "Been there. Done that," he said, hoping to deflect Luis' interest in Patterson with a bit of his personal trivia.

"Ah ha, that's a story that I would be interested in hearing," Luis laughed, the corners of his eyes crinkling in amusement. "Do I detect a hint of illicit behavior from a certain upstanding island businessman?"

"Maybe," Carlos grinned conspiratorially, "in a previous life, when I was young and foolish."

Luis leaned forward to whisper, "Maybe I should tell the beautiful Miss Yasmin about your exploits and she could include you in her novel. You could be the older and wiser knight in shining armor for her stunningly beautiful and naïve heroine." His eyebrows bounced playfully as he embellished his idea, "Or you could be the evil villain who ties the gorgeous heroine to the train tracks."

Laughing, Carlos held up his hands in a stop motion. "You are living in the past, *amigo*. Villains don't tie damsels in distress to train tracks anymore. Get with the new century." He shook a finger at Luis, "and you will not be telling my staff my personal secrets, or I will toss your skinny ass out onto the street and ban you from your favorite watering-hole."

The laughter suddenly disappearing from his voice, Luis' eyebrows scrunched in worry, creating a deep furrow in his forehead. "Seriously, what if it is the same guy?"

Crossing his arms over his chest, Carlos leaned against the back counter, "Leave it to me, I have a good friend in Mexico City who works for the Policía Federal. He's experienced," he said, before adding, "Unlike our local policía who are a bit over their heads when it comes to dealing with the really bad guys."

Chapter 21

November 11th Mid-afternoon

"Jesus, Kirk. You scared the hell out of us." Jessica snapped, holding her agitated dog. With a restraining hand on Sparky's chest, she could feel him vibrating with a deep growl. "What are you doing here?"

"I could ask you the same," he said, glaring at Jessica, his annoyance plainly written on his face. "Can't you shut that mutt up?"

"Shush, Sparky. It's okay." She stroked his head. "Don't worry baby. *No hay problema.*" Lowering the volume on his grumbling, Sparky locked his eyes on Kirk. "Good boy. Good boy." Jessica patted him again, unsettled over his reaction.

In his right hand, Kirk casually held an expensive looking Nikon camera, complete with a telephoto lens. "I was taking photographs of the old decaying structures—the stone benches, the wells, and the garden," he replied, his scrutiny lingering on the dog. "What are you two doing?"

"Hiking. Getting some exercise before we have to start work." Jessica tossed the words off casually, as if they were the truth. "You're a long way from the garden. It's down the hill, and in the center of the estate, not up here."

"I heard shouting. I thought someone needed help." Kirk's mouth twitched upward in a rictus of a smile as he tilted his chin towards Yasmin. "Looks like you are both okay though. What was the shouting about?" he added, an expression of curiosity on his face.

Searching his face, Jessica realized Kirk seemed to have gotten over his hissy fit from the other night, when he knocked over a chair and stormed out of the *Loco Lobo*. But right now, he had a flat stare and a smile that never quite reached his icy-blue eyes. *Creepy*.

Jessica answered his question before Yasmin could say anything, "Sparky was chasing an iguana. Yasmin shouted at him to stop." She glanced at Yasmin, hoping she would confirm the pretense.

"Yes, that's right." Yasmin nodded in agreement. "I told him to stop."

"There is a big crocodile that lives in the lake near the entrance. I didn't want Sparky getting too close to Alfredo...the crocodile," Jessica added offhandedly, thinking she didn't want to go into great detail about how Yasmin named the crocodile Alfredo instead of a something like Claudio, or Carl. *TMI*, she thought, *too much information*.

"Well it looks like everything is okay here." Kirk tipped his head towards Yasmin. "I'm heading back to the park entrance."

"Okay, thank you for checking on us," Yasmin quickly replied. "We're going to do a bit more hiking."

"Right. Nice footwear for hiking by the way," Kirk glanced down at Yasmin's beaded flip-flops, "so appropriate for tramping around in the woods with scorpions and snakes."

"We aren't exactly scrambling through the woods," Jessica retorted. "We are on a pathway and it's not steep. Yasmin's shoes are just fine." It wouldn't matter what he said, Jessica couldn't resist snapping out short-tempered comebacks.

Shrugging his shoulders indifferently, Kirk ambled away. "Sure, whatever you say."

Watching Kirk's retreating back, Jessica listlessly scuffed her foot in the soil a few more times, hoping to find another coin or two. "Damn him. Why does he always appear at the most inconvenient times?"

"It is a bit odd that he 'just happened'," Yasmin said, making air quotes with her fingers, "to be taking photographs today. We haven't seen a single person before, and now all of a sudden Kirk is here."

"We should be heading back. I have to feed the mutt-ski and get him settled for the evening." Jessica affectionately ruffled the dog's ears, thinking about how he had reacted to Kirk's sudden appearance. She remembered her dad always said a dog could sense danger. "Do you think Kirk has gone by now?"

"God I hope so. He's disturbing, isn't he? So good looking but so scary in a weird way." Yasmin shivered involuntarily, "I just don't like being around him."

"I know exactly what you mean. He lights up my bad-guy radar, big time," Jessica agreed.

Yasmin looked inquisitively at Jessica, "That sounds like the voice of experience. Did something bad happen to you?"

"Yeah, it's a long story." Jessica said as she gave Sparky's lead a gentle tug. "Come on boy, no more time for treasure hunting today. Let's head home." Jessica walked in silence, thinking about being a young girl and feeling threatened by an older man.

Carefully picking her way on the lumpy path, stepping over exposed tree roots and small rocks, Yasmin gently pressed Jessica for more information, "Do you feel like telling me your story?"

"Sure," Jessica said with a sigh. "I haven't thought about this in years. When I was about thirteen, I was asked to babysit for my auntie's friends. I didn't know them very well. They were at least ten years older than me." Reliving the memory in her mind, Jessica's eyes momentarily strayed away from the pathway. She flicked her gaze back to her feet when the toe of her sandal dislodged a small stone, causing her to stumble a little.

"Anyway," Jessica continued with her story, "around ten that night I was sitting on the sofa finishing my homework. The husband came home without his wife. He said he had to be at work early in the morning, but she wanted to stay at the party longer." She halted briefly while Sparky lifted his back leg, marking yet another bush. *This dog seemed to have a limitless supply of pee.*

Giving a small hurry-up tug on Sparky's harness, Jessica continued relating her story to Yasmin. "Then he suddenly sat beside me, pinning me against the arm of the sofa with his body. His right arm gripped my shoulders, and his left hand pressed on my thigh. He stared at me and asked, "Are you afraid?"

Jessica stopped walking. She stood, quietly collecting her thoughts for a few minutes. "I remember thinking I couldn't let him see that I was terrified, so I held his gaze. To this day, I clearly remember my reply, 'You are a police officer, and a member of the same Masonic Lodge that my father belongs to. I know nothing bad will happen to me.'"

"Oh, Jessica, how awful for you." Yasmin muttered, placing a hand on her friend's arm.

"I didn't move. I didn't blink. What seemed like an eternity later, he barked a short laugh and got up. He told me to get my stuff and he would drive me home." She shook her head, trying to dislodge the image of the leering man.

"Oh God, then what happened?" Yasmin said, following Jessica as she started down the path again, moving towards the gates.

"Nothing. He drove me to my house in complete silence. When I got out of the car, I didn't say goodbye or thank you or anything. I just shut the car door, and went inside my home."

"So he just left his kids alone while he took you home?"

"Yep. I think he was embarrassed by my reaction and just wanted to get me the hell out of the house." She cracked a wry smile, "I really hope that he didn't get a wink of sleep for months afterwards, wondering if I would tell someone about him."

"Did you tell anyone?"

"Sure, I told my auntie. She poo-pooed my concerns." Over the years Jessica had tried to forget the painful memory of her auntie's reaction. "She said he was a trusted policeman, a good friend, and a wonderful family man. She said I must have been mistaken and that I shouldn't stir up trouble for him or our family."

"Oh goodness." Yasmin said, "What about your mom and dad? Did you tell them?"

"No. It would be my word against the word of a police officer and a member of the Masonic Lodge. My dad loves me, but I just didn't want to cause any difficulties for him at his Lodge."

"Oh Jessica, I can't imagine how alone you must have felt."

Outside the park, they stopped beside Yasmin's red *Italika* moto. "Ever since then I have a fine-tuned bullshit radar." Jessica lifted Sparky into her arms, then slid onto the back seat of the moto, waiting while Yasmin found her ignition keys.

"Something is definitely off-kilter with Kirk Patterson. You need to be careful around him, Yasmin. Very careful."

Chapter 22

November 11th Late-afternoon

"Buenos Dias, Antonio," Carlos said, leaning back into his comfortable leather chair as he chatted with his boyhood friend who now worked in Mexico City. "I hope all is well with you." He glanced through his office window towards the restaurant, mentally counting the number of customers enjoying their alcohol-inspired I'm-on-vacation drinks. He smiled broadly when he saw a striking young woman strut into the bar wearing a skimpy thong bikini. *Whew. Great ass.* Ya gotta love working in a popular tourist destination where the visitors were carefree and uninhibited, especially the good-looking women.

Momentarily distracted by the sight of an overweight middle-aged man wearing only a bright green banana hammock that barely covered his genitals, Carlos nearly missed Antonio's question. *Good god; that was a vision he could have done without.* "Si, I am well. Everything is good. Si." He straightened up, resting well-muscled forearms on the big desk, "I have a favor to ask, amigo."

At the other end of the conversation, Capitan Antonio Martinez, of the Policía Federal, sputtered, "*Pendejo*. Why do you only call me when you want a favor? Can you not call just to find out if I am well, or if my wife and children still love me, or if I am getting enough sex from my mistress?"

Laughing aloud, Carlos retorted, "You always get enough sex from your mistress, otherwise she becomes your ex-mistress number thirty-five, or is it number thirty-six? Why does your sweet wife, Luisa, put up with you? She is a saint, and you are the devil incarnate."

Antonio really was one of the good guys. Carlos thought, not for the first time and probably not for the last time, that he really should take the time to visit him. Maybe fly out and spend a week eating, drinking and reminiscing with his long-time friend. Life was short, but for a prominent cop like Antonio, it could be very dangerous and very short. Carlos relished time spent with Antonio, Luisa and their amazing brood of kids. If all kids came with a guarantee that they would be as funny, smart, and lovable as Luisa's youngsters, he wouldn't mind one or two himself, one day.

"Pah, my Luisa adores me. I am a god-fearing family man," Antonio retorted good-naturedly.

"What do you want this time?" Through the phone, Carlos could hear the sound of Antonio's wide fingers mashing the computer keyboard, probably logging into the secure information system.

"A little information of course. A friend of mine mentioned he had seen news articles about a murderer in Florida. Some sick jerk who used GHB to drug and rape a young woman, then slit her throat. Do you know anything about him?" Troubled by the thought of Yasmin or any of the island's young women being in danger, Carlos restlessly ran his hand through his short dark hair as he quizzed Antonio. "My friend also said the suspect had shoulder-length dark brown hair and a beard, although both of those could easily be changed."

"A murderer loose in America. Oh, my goodness, what a surprise." Antonio's cynicism was apparent in his tone of voice. "At any given day there are anywhere from forty to fifty people murdered in America, and those my friend are the recent stats from the FBI's Crime Unit. Why are you interested in one particular killer in Florida?"

Carlos could hear the hard, inquisitive-cop edge in Antonio's voice. "Just curious. A local friend thought he had seen a tourist on Isla Mujeres that resembled the suspect on the Florida news programs. You have any photographs? A description or a name?"

"Si, of course. I, Capitan Juan Antonio Martinez Garcia would be delighted to be of service to you. Once again I will risk my very good-paying job and my exalted station in life to assist a reformed hoodlum with his inquiries."

Amused, Carlos reminded Antonio that they were both reformed hoodlums; one of whom was able to erase his shady past through family connections in the Policía Federal, and a bit of creative hacking in the national computer system, while he, Carlos, had learned to live with the memory of his mistakes.

"Yeah, whatever." Antonio rattled the keys in quick succession, typing in the search parameters of murder, rape, GHB, and Florida. The screen listed four possibilities. He quickly scanned the list, discounting three because one was dead, one was locked up, and the third was too old. He guessed the fourth one was probably the person that Carlos was interested in. "Same email address as before?" Antonio asked.

"Yes."

"Okay, give me a few minutes and then I'll pop the file to you. If this is the guy, you call me back *pronto*. Agreed?"

Carlos said with a sardonic laugh in his voice, "Why? What can you do about it?"

152

"I can light a fire under someone's butt in that *pequeño pueblo* that you call home, and get his sorry ass tossed in jail."

"Sure, sure. Luis and I will check the photos and we'll let you know."

"Okay gotta go, got more bad guys to lock up. Adios *pendejo*."

"Gracias. Give my love to Luisa." Carlos' finger hovered near the disconnect button, waiting for Antonio to finish talking.

"Nope. Call her yourself. She is always asking about you." Mimicking a younger female voice, Antonio teased his friend. "When's Carlos coming for a visit? What is Carlos doing? Is Carlos married yet?" Switching back to his own voice, he asked, "Should I be worried?"

"No. You own a gun, a really big gun, with lots of bullets. Adios, bud."

Ten minutes later an email with an attachment landed in Carlos' inbox. He downloaded and opened the file. "Well, well, what a bad little boy you have been, Kirk," he muttered, "or should I call you the name you used in Florida—Kyle Johnson?" He printed off the photograph showing Kirk's face, with longer collar-length hair and a beard.

"Suspected of one, maybe two, rapes and murders in the Florida Keys. What a nasty piece of work." Carlos folded the printout into his pocket and picked up the keys to his 911-S Porsche. Time to call in a few favors from his past.

Chapter 23

November 12th Middle of the night

It was late, long after midnight, when Jessica had returned home from work and taken Sparky out for his nighttime pee-walk. They had taken their usual slow amble around the block as the dog investigated every power pole, bush and tree — reapplying his mark over those left by previous male dogs. *How could one small dog hold that much fluid in his bladder?*

Finally settling in for the night, Jessica relaxed, sipping on a glass of cold Sauvignon Blanc. It was a decent one from New Zealand, not the acidic, mouth-puckering cheap stuff she usually bought. She let her mind wander over the events of the last ten days: first the drunken, ill-conceived graveyard raid on Mundaca's tomb, then the futile search for the treasure in his abandoned house, then searching the mosquito-infested land at Sac Bajo, and finally tramping around the small hills behind Mundaca's estate, twice. All this while working six days a week, and trying to avoid Ryan and that weirdo Kirk, and oh yeah, any cops or government officials that might wonder what the hell they were up to.

Other than the boat ride a few nights ago, she and Yasmin hadn't had any after-hours fun for so long she forgot what it was like to feel an alcohol buzz. Annoyed, she puffed upwards, momentarily blowing her sweat-dampened bangs off her forehead. Even in mid-November the temperatures were still too warm for her northern blood.

Leaning against her leg, Sparky looked up, his dark brown eyes seeking hers. His thick terrier eyebrows were stitched into an impression of a frown. Jessica reached down and affectionately rubbed his ears. "Don't worry, little man. I'm just tired, and frustrated."

She twirled one of the dull gold coins on the table, wondering if they would be able to keep them. Pretty difficult to know for sure without revealing that they were treasure hunting, without a permit, which according to the *notario* Luis Aguilar was impossible to obtain anyway. She was fairly certain that if they alerted the authorities, a government official would confiscate the coins, toss her and Yasmin in jail, and then keep the loot for himself.

Maybe she was being a little cynical, but that was the impression that she got from Yasmin whenever they talked about the treasure. Corruption was a way of life for politicians and government officials in most countries. In the USA, or even her own supposedly corruption-free country of Canada, it was better disguised, but there all the same.

Looking down at Sparky, Jessica smiled. "Well we tried to turn you into a treasure locating hound, but there should have been more, lots more. I wonder why you didn't find the other coins." She leaned over and lightly scratched his chest, "No worries, you are still a good doggie, and I love you." Sparky's dark brown eyes stared at her, and his tongue lolled out of the side of his mouth as he thumped his tail. He seemed to be agreeing with her.

"Okay, bud, let's head to bed. Tomorrow is another day." She glanced at the time displayed on her iPhone, "Two in the morning, so, today is already here. Bedtime." She patted her leg, and Sparky followed her into the tiny bedroom, his nails clicking a light tattoo on the tiles.

An hour later her cell erupted into the Crazy Frog ding Ing song, her current and increasingly annoying ring tone. "That better not be a wrong number," she moaned as she fumbled to answer the phone. "Hola?"

"Jessica! I need help!" Yasmin's frantic voice blasted through the tiny speaker.

Sitting up abruptly, Jessica could feel her pulse start to race. "Yasmin, what's wrong?"

"Someone is trying to break into my house."

"Call the police!" Jessica leapt out of bed, hopping on one foot and fumbling with her shorts, as she kept the phone tucked between her ear and shoulder.

"No. They're no help."

"Then call Carlos."

"No. I don't want to wake him up."

"Hang on! I'll be there in ten minutes." She clipped Sparky's leash to his collar, grabbed her keys and phone, and rushed out, locking the door behind her. Walking quickly towards Yasmin's place, Jessica searched her phone for Carlos' contact information.

His sleep-roughened voice answered. "Bueno?"

"This is Jessica. Yasmin needs help." On the other end of the conversation, Jessica could hear fumbling noises. Carlos' voice was slightly muffled as if he had the phone tucked under his chin while he pulled on his clothes.

"What happened?"

"She said someone is trying to break into her house. She's terrified."

Swearing loudly in expressive Spanish, Carlos told Jessica that he would get there as quickly as possible. "Take your dog, and make lots of noise, but be careful."

"Okay," Jessica replied, puffing slightly, "Sparky and I are here now at her house. She disconnected the call, "Yasmin, where are you?"

"Here, just inside the door," came the timid voice. "I couldn't decide if I was safer inside, or out on the street."

Sniffing the sidewalk and entrance area, Sparky began to growl, tugging hard on his leash as he tried to follow a scent trail. "No, Sparky, no. Stay. We need you here boy," Jessica said, straining to keep the tough little dog from dragging her with him.

The women turned towards the roar of a high-performance sports car approaching their neighborhood. They heard the squeal of brakes and a scrape of the undercarriage as the car slammed over an unmarked *tope* at the entrance to their street, then the Porsche stopped abruptly at Yasmin's entrance. Carlos flung open the car door and swung his legs to the sidewalk.

Standing just inside the front door, Jessica sketched a small wave at Carlos. Her other arm was wrapped around Yasmin's shoulders, comforting her.

Agitated, Sparky barked sharply. "*Tranquilo,* Sparky," Jessica cautioned him. "Carlos is a friend."

Carlos waited for a few seconds while the dog sniffed his pant leg before advancing towards the women. "Yasmin, what happened?"

"Carlos, I...I...didn't want Jessica to wake you." She stuttered as her body shook with tremors.

He smiled grimly, "Don't worry about me. Just tell me what happened."

Yasmin's teeth clicked together, "Why am I so cold?"

"You've had a bad scare. It's the after-effects of adrenaline. It'll pass in a few minutes."

Yasmin pulled away from Jessica, her trembling slowly subsiding. "I was sleeping, and I heard a noise at my front door. Then I heard what sounded like my kitchen table scraping on the tile floor, like someone had bumped into it. I started yelling, hoping to scare the person away."

"Did you get a look at the intruder?"

"No. I barricaded my bedroom door with my dresser and pushed against it while I called Jessica." She shivered again at the memory. "I'm pretty sure it was only one guy and that my yelling scared him off."

"Smart." Carlos nodded, adding, "There's really no point calling the police. They don't have fingerprinting equipment and they have very little training for crime scene investigations." Examining the door lock, he added, "This is a cheap piece of hardware. Let's just get your house secured for the night and worry about a proper repair in the morning." He turned to look at the women, "You should both stay here for the night, with me, and the dog. Just in case this guy is still in the neighborhood."

"No, we'll be fine at Jessica's." Yasmin answered, "I want to get away from here for a few hours."

"Then I'll come with you to Jessica's."

"No, please Carlos. We'll be fine, but I am a bit worried about my things," she said, looking uncertainly at her living space. "My door can't be locked."

Carlos stood out in the middle of the street, apprehensively watching the two women and the dog as they turned into Jessica's house. It wasn't the best solution, but it was what Yasmin was comfortable with.

His cell rang. Yasmin said, "We are here Carlos, at Jessica's."

"I know. I was watching. Lock the doors," he said, walking towards Yasmin's. "Call me right away if you have any problems.

"Yes, of course. And thank you so much, again." She whispered, "Good night Carlos."

"Good night, Yasmin." He replied softly, then clicked the end call button, pensively regarding his phone.

When he had arrived and seen Yasmin's frightened face, it had been very difficult not to enfold her in his arms. Now, thinking about holding Yasmin tight to his chest, he suddenly noticed a musty odor radiating from his shirt. He lifted his arm and turned his head to sniff in the region of his armpits. It was the same shirt he had worn all day at work. Great. Just great. Hopefully, she hadn't noticed that he smelled like an old bear. There hadn't been any time to fuss about personal hygiene.

Inside the house, Carlos pulled the door closed; it would help keep the mosquitoes at bay while he babysat the house. A glint of gold caught his eye from behind the door. Reaching, he picked up a chain with a broken clasp. A shark's tooth dangled from it. "*Madre de Dios*! That settles it. That *pendejo* Kirk was wearing something similar a few days ago," Carlos muttered as he pulled two kitchen chairs close together. He plunked down on one and propped his feet on the other.

Thumbing through his phone contacts, he rang a familiar number, "Diego. It's me, Carlos."

"Hey, bud." A sleepy voice answered, yawning. "Do you know what time it is?"

"Si, I know it's three in the morning. That *pendejo* we discussed earlier? We need to speed things up a bit."

"What happened?" Diego sounded wide-awake now.

Running the gold chain through his fingers, Carlos answered. "He scared the hell out of Yasmin tonight. Tried to break into her house."

"That's not good. Pedro and I will deal with it tomorrow."

A hard look crossed Carlos' face as he listened to Diego. "Remember, no policía."

Chapter 24

November 12th Three in the morning

Leaning back in the shadows, Kirk stared intently at the black Porsche crouched at the curb by Yasmin's house. He could feel his pulse hammer in his carotid artery, thumping with the beat of his heart, not fast but forceful. His rage was under control, barely. He savored the heightened awareness of the adrenaline rushing through his veins. A slowing down of time. A crystallization of events.

After he had left the two women in the park, he had powered on the Nikon and quickly scrolled through his photos. Those two lying bitches had found something small and metal. Thumbing the user control wheel, he was able to zoom in on the item that Jessica was holding. It looked like a coin, a gold coin. Ryan had told him that Jessica blabbed something about pirate treasure. In the camera viewfinder she'd looked pretty damn excited about whatever they had found, so maybe, just maybe, that buried treasure story was real.

He'd come prepared to search the house for the coins. He had plans for scooping up anything he found and disappearing, alone, to yet another Caribbean island, preferably one without an extradition agreement with either the USA or Mexico. Things could get a little messy before he left Isla, and he didn't plan to be dragged back to rot in a stinking Mexican jail. Unfortunately, that bitch Yasmin had heard him breach her flimsy door lock and she'd kicked up an almighty commotion. Between the yelling and screaming she had managed to call the blond for help. Then one of them had called that interfering bastard Carlos, who came flying up the street in his fancy sports car.

It was obvious to him now that Carlos had a thing for Yasmin. He was very protective of her. It was probably Carlos who had pulled that back alley stunt a few days ago, using a chokehold to render him unconscious. *No worries*, Kirk smirked, *he might think he's a tough guy, but he doesn't have the guts to just take what he wants. Instead he plays around at being all polite and gentlemanly. Too bad for you loser, I'm going to get what I want.* Leave her alive or not, he hadn't quite made up his mind on that. The odds were fifty-fifty at the moment.

And then there was that noisy mutt that Jessica dragged everywhere. Even though the dog was short and about the size of a Beagle, he looked tough and capable of biting, hard. Kirk had never been a fan of dogs, they seemed to instinctively dislike him. The dog had gone ballistic when he picked up his scent at Yasmin's front door. He probably remembered Kirk from when he had deliberately 'bumped into' Yasmin and Jessica at the park.

He pressed the switchblade closed. Guns might be illegal in Mexico, but most of the local fishermen and construction workers carried knives. The cops didn't pay any attention to the bulge in his front pocket.

Kirk watched Carlos through the front window as he pulled two chairs together and settled in to wait for daylight. He seemed to be shifting something shiny from hand to hand. Kirk's hand instinctively reached for his neck. Gone. His signature gold chain with the attached shark's tooth was missing.

He carefully removed a pair of latex surgical gloves from his hands, stuffing them in the back pocket of his jeans along with the plastic flexi-cuffs.

Okay then, Plan A didn't work out. Plan B it is.

Chapter 25

November 12th Mid-day

"Good morning Carlos," Yasmin said, answering her phone. "I mean good afternoon, since it's already noon."

"Did I wake you?"

"No, no. We're up. Are you still at my place?" she asked, feeling guilty about leaving him to sort out her problems in the middle of the night.

"No, I'm at my place, getting cleaned up for work. Your casita has a nice new door, and a better lock. Your windows already had security bars, so you should be fine now."

"I had the security bars installed because I like to sleep with the windows open and didn't want to worry about an intruder." She laughed derisively, then continued. "I guess I should have thought about a better door lock at the same time."

"It's all taken care of now. Why don't you and Jessica take the day off? I'll get someone else to cover your shift," Carlos offered.

Yasmin thought for a minute, then said, "No thank you, we're fine. We managed to get enough sleep last night. We'll be in at our regular time."

Saying goodbye and disconnecting the call, Yasmin stared at the kitchen table, thinking.

"You okay now?" Jessica asked, as she poured herself a cup of coffee.

"Yes, I'm fine," Yasmin said. "I'm sorry for being such a baby last night."

"Hey no worries, that's what friends are for."

"Now I'm angry, really angry at the low-life who violated my home," she said, her face stiff with tension.

"Why don't you adopt a dog, for protection?" Jessica asked, jiggling the coffee carafe from side to side, to get Yasmin's attention. "Want more? I need this stuff to get my heart started when I wake up."

"Sure," she said, holding her cup out for Jessica to refill. "Thanks." Ignoring Jessica's question about getting a dog, Yasmin took another swig of the dark-roasted brew. "I refuse to let a thief make me afraid to live by myself."

Jessica stirred a little skim milk into her cup. "So, why don't you get a dog?"

"You know how I feel about dogs in the house. It's the way I was brought up." Yasmin finger-combed her sleep-rumpled hair. "Besides, I don't have a yard and I'm not going to let a pet sleep out on the street. It just wouldn't work for me."

"But you like Sparky." Jessica grinned, patting him as she spoke. "We know Yasmin likes you, don't we boy?" Sparky's tail swished back and forth like a single windshield wiper sweeping the floor.

Yasmin's stiff expression relaxed as she looked at Sparky. "I admit it, I do, but he's the only dog that I know." She added sheepishly, "Besides, I haven't got a clue how to look after one."

"Ah, so it's a maybe." Pulling a silly face, Jessica scratched Sparky's curly head. "We can teach her, can't we Sparky?" Jessica straightened up and rested her hip against the kitchen counter. "Okay, the dog issue aside, what are we going to do now about finding this treasure? I'm completely out of ideas."

"No kidding. Me too." Yasmin huffed. "But the Hacienda Mundaca area still seems the most promising. After all that's where you and your famous ore-sniffing dog found the coins." She pointed at Sparky, smiling at the irony of the situation. She had thought Jessica was nuts when she rescued the dirty bug-infested mutt, but the tough little guy was proving to be very useful, and if she was forced to admit it, very sweet.

"Three coins, out of seventy thousand. Not exactly the mother lode."

"True, but it's something, and if we actually can cash them in...well, who knows? A least we know the hoard might actually exist."

Jessica turned around and rinsed out her coffee cup under the kitchen faucet. "Should we try again near that collapsed cave entrance? Although, I'm beginning to agree with your idea of using a metal detector to hunt for the treasure."

Yasmin shook her head. "No, you were right. It would draw too much attention to us. People would ask awkward questions." Considering their options, Yasmin looked at Jessica's dog. "Oh hell, what have we got to lose? Let's give *el Chispa* one more chance tomorrow to find the loot, and if that doesn't work, well, I have no idea where to search next."

Remembering something she had overhead the day before, something about a week of bad weather, Jessica flicked the screen of her iPhone, bringing up the Intellicast weather for Cancun and Isla Mujeres. "Aw, rats. There's a storm headed this way. Lots of rain and wind over the next five to seven days."

"Really?" Yasmin grabbed her phone and checked a different weather site. "That's late in the season. We are usually done with the risk of storms by now."

Shaking her head in disagreement, Jessica said, "Nope, according to the National Hurricane Center, the Atlantic season is from June 1st to November 30th. We are still in mid-November."

"Never mind, it probably won't amount to anything. Storms have a habit of veering off towards Cuba or dissipating unexpectedly." Yasmin studied the webpage showing the predicted track for the weather system, centering over Isla Mujeres then advancing north across the Gulf of Mexico towards Florida. She shrugged; that was a pretty normal route for a storm. "It isn't due to hit Isla until late tomorrow night. We'll be done and gone to work by then."

Chapter 26

November 12ᵗʰ Mid-day

Ryan wiped a French fry across his empty
plate, scraping up the last of the juice from his huge
double-patty cheeseburger. He patted his bulging
stomach. He was stuffed, but it had tasted so damn
good. It was a nice change from tortillas, tacos, and
quesadillas. He enjoyed Mexican food, just not every
day. Sometimes he just craved good old American
chow—cheeseburgers and cold beer. Good tunes
played in the background, loud enough to hear, but
not so loud he couldn't chat with the other bar
patrons.

Tilting his head back, Ryan contemplated the
wacky collection of baseball-style caps, licence
plates, and other memorabilia from various places in
the USA and Canada. The assortment grew every
day as returning visitors dropped into their favorite
island beach bar, stapling their hometown souvenirs
to the wooden crossbeams of the palapa. *Wonder
what the hell they do with all this stuff when there's*

a hurricane? Lost in thought, he didn't notice as a tall, rangy man entered the bar.

"Hey, I noticed your rental scooter outside. I decided to join you." Kirk slid onto the bar stool next to Ryan, signalling the bartender at the Soggy Peso Bar for a cold Sol. He carefully set his expensive Nikon camera on the bar, along with his Maui Jim sunglasses.

Startled, Ryan's eyebrows popped up. "Hey yourself, Kirk. Where have you been? I haven't seen you around lately."

Nodding at the bartender, Kirk tipped back the cold beer and swallowed several times. He placed the half-empty bottle back on the bar and shrugged his shoulders. "Been busy taking lots of photographs. What about you? What have you been up to?"

"Not a lot. A bit of kitesurfing, hanging around on Playa Norte checking out the thong bikinis. The usual." He grinned, then ordered two more cold Sols, indicating to the bartender that one was for Kirk.

"Thanks for the beer." Kirk drained his first one and pushed the empty bottle out of his way. He turned his flat gaze on Ryan.

Feeling as if he was undergoing an inspection, Ryan shifted uncomfortably on the bar stool. He felt like a bug held under a microscope. Kirk appeared to be making up his mind about something.

Nodding as if he had come to a decision, Kirk picked up his camera and thumbed the control wheel, flicking through his photographs. He looked coolly at Ryan. "I'll show you something, but you need to keep quiet about it," he said with a hint of menace in his voice, waiting for Ryan's answer.

"Sure. What is it?" Ryan leaned towards the camera display screen, thinking maybe Kirk was going to show him photographs of nude beach babes. The guy seemed to have a seriously kinky side to his personality. Squinting at the digital photograph, he couldn't quite make out what Jessica was holding in her hand, and why it was so important. "What the hell am I looking at?" He asked, in a confused tone.

Kirk cast a glance around, checking to see who was nearby. "It's a coin."

"Okay? And that means what exactly?" Ryan was still puzzled.

"I maximized the image on my laptop. That is a very old, possibly Spanish, gold coin." He waited for Ryan to grasp the significance.

"Damn it! I knew it." Ryan barked, slapping the bar counter causing his beer bottle to jiggle with the force of the blow. "They have been up to something for the last two weeks."

"Shut up man," Kirk hissed as he noticed the bar staff looking at them quizzically.

As he picked up his beer, Ryan's hands were shaking with excitement. "Yeah, sorry about that. I just got a little overexcited. I've been following those two on my rental moto for several days trying to figure out what they are up to." He slurped a gulp of beer, trying to calm his nerves. "Spanish treasure."

"I said, Shut. Up. I'm seriously beginning to regret telling you."

"Yeah, yeah. I said I was sorry." Ryan's brain buzzed as if he had consumed two cans of Red Bull high-energy drink. This was all too much to grasp. Treasure. Wow. Un-freaking-believable! "So, now what? Do we offer to help dig it up?"

Kirk's cold blue eyes contemplated Ryan. "No. We don't offer to help. We just wait and keep an eye on them. We'll offer our assistance once we think they have located everything possible."

Acid squirted into Ryan's stomach, ruining his lunch, as he thought about what Kirk had said, and more importantly how he had said it. Why did he continue to hang around with this cold bastard?

Later, as the tall gringo and the shorter blond-haired guy left the bar, a well-dressed Latino made a scribbling motion in the air with his right hand, signalling for his bill. He'd been sitting quietly at the bar reading the news on his iPad when he noticed the two men chatting to his left. He had seen them several times at the *Loco Lobo* and thought about saying hello, but soon realized they were discussing something privately and wouldn't appreciate his interruption. He'd heard the blond one shout something about Spanish treasure. Interesting. It was definitely worth keeping an eye on them.

Walking out of the bar, he browsed his phone's contact list, clicked on a number, and waited patiently until the call was answered.

"This is Jorge. I have a job for you. Meet me at the office in twenty minutes."

Chapter 27

November 13ᵗʰ Early morning

The morning sun was obscured by a heavy layer of dark grey clouds, forcing Jessica to turn on her kitchen light while making her morning coffee. As she opened the door to her tiny backyard, the wind slammed the door against the inside wall. Sparky slid between her legs, running to the postage-stamp sized piece of lawn. "Pees and poops. *Rápido. Rápido.*" She grabbed at the door to prevent the handle from banging against the wall again. No sense irritating her landlord with unnecessary repairs.

Rechecking the weather forecast and the NOAA—National Oceanic and Atmospheric Administration—hurricane sites, Jessica impatiently waited for the coffee maker to finish its job. "Damn it. Now, the rain is forecast to arrive early this afternoon. Ugh. Oh well, maybe the rain will help us uncover more treasure."

Twenty minutes later, dressed in jeans and a t-shirt, Jessica heard Yasmin arrive on her *Italika* moto. Yasmin walked in, carrying two bright yellow rain slickers crumpled in one hand.

Pointing at the coats, Jessica laughed. "Don't you have any black plastic garbage bags to use as a raincoat?" she said, referring to the local habit of slicing a hole in the end of a large plastic bag and slipping it on when the weather turned wet.

"I wouldn't be caught dead wearing one of those." Yasmin reached for an empty cup, helping herself to some of Jessica's freshly made coffee. "Oh, God, that is so good." She briefly closed her eyes, enjoying the aroma and the taste of the dark brew. "We might need these coats later this morning." She sipped the coffee again, then continued, "My neighbor, Ernesto, is a lobster fisherman, and he saw me getting on my moto holding the raincoats. He teased me that I'd need something better than thin plastic to keep dry today. According to him the rain is arriving earlier than forecasted."

"Okay, drink up, and let's get at it," Jessica said, rinsing her cup under the tap. "We can still have a look around the park and be home before the rain hits."

Yasmin reluctantly took one last large gulp, pouring the remainder down the sink.

Jessica bent and clipped the harness on Sparky, then attached his leash to the D-ring. "Okay, bud. All set to find us more treasure?" Reaching for the rain slicker and her keys, Jessica scooped up a small cloth bag that was hanging on the handle of her kitchen door. *This might come in handy.* She let Yasmin go out first, then turned and locked the door behind her.

Yasmin scrunched her eyebrows. "I wish we could take a shovel or something with us. Just kicking our sandals in the dirt doesn't accomplish much."

Jessica smiled and pointed at Sparky. "We have a shovel right here. Look at those two front feet. Haven't you ever noticed that they are bigger than his back paws? He's built for digging."

Glancing down at the dog's feet, Yasmin said, "You're right. I never noticed before. Maybe you should have named him Digger." Yasmin hopped onto the moto, patting the seat behind her. "Come on pooch, you have earned a ride with us."

Arriving back at the entrance to the Hacienda Mundaca Park, the attendant at the gate recognized the two women and the dog. "Come to give the crocodile another chance at your dog?" Adela taunted Jessica while taking their entrance fees and applying the paper wrist bands. "What is so fascinating here that you keep coming back?"

Unable to think up a snappy and plausible excuse, Yasmin blushed, averting her eyes, while Jessica quickly retorted. "Hiking. We like to exercise before going to work. Keeps us fit."

"Sure, that makes sense, I guess." The woman didn't look convinced, but she didn't question them any further. "Well, you know your way around. Keep in mind there is a storm coming soon and the pathways get really slippery when it rains," she smiled wryly, "and we wouldn't want you falling near the lake. The crocodile might roll you up like a burrito and stuff you into the mud to age a bit before he eats you." She chuckled at her own wit.

Yasmin rolled her eyes and walked up the pathway, "Gracias, Doña Adela," she said, her voice heavy with sarcasm.

Jessica and Sparky slowly followed behind as he sniffed at and peed on every bush. "Jeesh, Sparky, don't you ever run out of liquid? Come on pooch, we don't have a lot of time before the storm arrives. *Vámonos*."

Chapter 28

November 13th Mid-morning

A grin splitting her wide, round face, Adela watched as the two young women and the short mutt disappeared into the jungle. It was fun to tease the blond one about the crocodile. She was very protective of her dog, like a mother with a toddler.

Turning at the sound of another motor-scooter arriving, Adela noticed two *gringo* men striding towards the entrance; one had dark hair, the other was blond. She waited until they were about to enter the park, thinking they would stop and ask if there was an admission price, but the taller one appeared to be intent on powering past her. "Thirty pesos each, please," she said politely, holding out a hand to stop them from passing by.

The tall man dug in his front pocket pulling out a hundred peso note. "Here. Keep the change." He abruptly handed her the money as he continued to walk.

"Wait please, Señor." Adela held up a hand in a stop motion. "You have to have a wrist band to show that you have paid your entrance fee."

"Oh, for Christ sake!" The tall one stopped mid-stride and impatiently stuck out his arm, all the while craning his neck to keep the two women in sight.

"So, are those pretty ladies friends of yours?" Adela asked, her dark brown eyes crinkling with mischief as she winked playfully.

"No." The angry one snapped impatiently.

"Yes." The other man replied simultaneously with a lopsided smile.

Bemused, Adela lifted an eyebrow, "No. Yes. Someone's confused."

"Whatever." The dark-haired man stormed past her, headed along the pathway, while the shorter blond man trailed along behind him.

Perplexed, she looked after the two men. *What the heck was that all about?*

Even more perplexing was that a few minutes later, two more men arrived at the entrance. They were both slightly familiar looking although she didn't know their names. They were well-muscled and had a hard edge to their movements. One of the men had a nose that had been broken, and badly reset, more than a few times. She recognized the look, as her first husband had been a brawler. The other one looked just as tough with his shaved head and part of a tattoo poking out from his left shirtsleeve. The taller man carried a heavy looking black backpack in his right hand.

A small tremor of uncertainty ran down her spine as she silently accepted the entrance fees from the grim-faced men. "Gracias," she said as the older of the two politely dipped his head in a thank you gesture, then strode purposefully up the pathway in the direction of the previous four people.

Stepping into the small shelter at the park entrance, Adela toyed with her phone. How very odd that so many people were entering the park when a storm was forecast to arrive soon. Something was amiss. *Should she call someone? But who? Her boss at the Palacio Municipal? The Policía?* She didn't want to be laughed at for being a silly woman. *What could she really tell them? Two women and four men came into the park, and then what?* Unsettled, Adela checked the time, then put her phone back in her pocket.

One hour. If she didn't see the women returning in one hour, she would call her boss.

While Adela stared after the recent arrivals, a man dressed in tan chinos and a white short-sleeved shirt eased through the employee entrance, a simple wooden gate located behind the animal clinic. He quickly trotted along the familiar pathway leading around the lake, towards the sound of a young woman chiding a dog for walking too slowly.

Chapter 29

November 13th Mid-morning

Sparky stopped abruptly, turning his head to look behind. His nose tilted upwards as he sniffed the air, licking his nose a few times to enhance his ability to smell. Jessica tugged gently on his leash, but the stocky little mutt planted his feet and refused to budge. "Come on, bud. We don't have time to mess around." She pulled harder. "Come. On." Reluctantly Sparky followed her, turning his head several times to look.

Yasmin tilted her head up as she heard a distant rumble of thunder. "That storm is moving in quicker than we thought. Maybe we should leave this for another day?" The wind gusted, swirling fallen leaves into the air.

"It is supposed to rain hard for the next five days. We're here. We might as well have a look." Jessica continued to stride deeper into the park, headed back towards the small cave higher up the hill. It was there at the entrance that Sparky had uncovered the three Spanish coins.

The dog stopped again, turning to look behind. "Sparky, what is wrong with you? Are you afraid of the thunder?" Jessica asked impatiently. They didn't have a lot of time before the rain started, and she really wanted to search for more of the Spanish doubloons. She wasn't worried about the thunder, but the rain could make the path treacherous, and riding home on the moto in a downpour would be very uncomfortable, especially navigating through the flooded intersections of the badly maintained streets.

"Don't worry, nothing will happen to you. Come on pooch. Let's get moving." A light patter of rain started to fall, plinking off the jungle leaves and dampening the ground.

Yasmin and Jessica pulled on the bright yellow rain slickers, fastening the snaps down the front. Yasmin's sandal slid on the damp ground. She reached out to steady herself against a small tree. "Jeesh, this is getting slippery. As much as I hate to admit it, Kirk was right, I should be wearing better shoes for tramping around in the woods."

"No worries, we are almost there. Come on Sparky, do your thing. *Buscar. Buscar.*" Jessica urged the little dog as she unclipped his harness, "Find us some gold, sweet boy."

Nose to the ground, Sparky swept back and forth across the pathway, ignoring the increasing noise from the thunder and the occasional flash of distant lightning. The rain increased in volume, gathering up the dry soil into little dust-coated droplets that gathered speed, melding into little rivulets headed down the hill towards the lake. Oblivious to the rain, Sparky's sensitive nose finally picked up on a scent that he recognized. He stopped and pawed gently at the earth. Sticking his nose into the small depression he had created, he inhaled deeply, and pawed again. One sharp bark, and he sat down.

"Seriously? Good boy Sparky. Let's see what you found." Kneeling on the wet ground, Jessica playfully dug into the earth, encouraging Sparky to play his favorite game. "Are there crabs in here? I think there are crabs in here. Come on boy, help find the crabs." The dog enthusiastically dug in the increasingly rain-soaked dirt. "Crabs. Let's get the crabs." A gold coin flew out of the small hole and tumbled down the path a short distance. "Yasmin, grab that coin!"

A distance away, hidden in the thick jungle undergrowth, Kirk and Ryan heard Jessica shout, *"Grab that coin."*

"They've found something. Let's get a little closer," Kirk said, impatiently motioning for Ryan to hurry up. A lightning strike lit up the sky, with an instantaneous ear-splitting crash of thunder. The storm had arrived.

"This is turning really nasty." Ryan wiped the rain from his eyes, his soaking wet clothes stuck to his body. "Let's go back."

Turning to look at Ryan, Kirk's lips curled in a sneer. "Is the little boy getting wet? Maybe you should run home to momma."

"Jesus, Kirk, we can't see anything. It's a freaking tropical storm."

"Ryan, get the hell out of here. You're useless."

"Yeah, well screw you too!" Ryan turned around and stumbled down the pathway, sliding in the gooey mud, landing on his tailbone with a curse. He scrambled to his feet, favouring his left leg. His knee had twisted under his body as he landed in the muck. "Great." As he limped down the path, another series of simultaneous lightning strikes and thunderclaps shook the ground, rattling the trees. Startled, Ryan lost his balance, landed hard, and rolled off the pathway. Unable to stop his slide, he whacked his head against a rock. With a groan he sank into the mud, hidden beneath the thick undergrowth.

"Jessica this is ridiculous. We have to go back!" Yasmin yelled over the fury of the lightning and thunder.

"Wait, just another minute. I think Sparky has found more coins," she shouted, certain that no one would overhear. No one else would be crazy enough to be out in this storm. The rain pounded down on her head and shoulders, turning the ground where she knelt to a chocolate brown river. It made excavating the dirt easier, but it was also harder to see what Sparky was digging up. She felt around in the ooze, touching several small objects. *Yes.* The storm was actually helping uncover the treasure. Jessica stuffed the mud-covered articles into the cloth bag that she had brought with her. A bolt of lightning sizzled through the air, causing the hairs on her arms to stand up; then not a heartbeat later the thunder crashed overhead. "Okay, that was close. Okay, let's get out of here before we get zapped by lightning."

Sparky suddenly let out a vicious growl and bared his fangs. Frightened, Jessica instinctively grabbed the dog's harness, as a dark figure cinched a muscular arm across Yasmin's throat.

"I'll take that," Kirk yelled, nodding in the direction of the sack that Jessica held in her hands. He calmly held a knife under Yasmin's chin, forcing her head back. As the sharp blade pushed against her skin, a thin rivulet of blood slid down her throat.

Terror expanded the pupils of Yasmin's eyes. She stared at Jessica, silently begging for help.

Chapter 30

November 13th Late-morning

"Kirk! You son-of-a-bitch." Jessica screamed, her eyes sparking with rage. "Let her go!" Sparky slashed the air with exposed fangs, trying desperately to launch himself at the intruder.

"Give me that sack or I'll cut her throat."

"Bastard!" Her hand wrapped tightly around Sparky's lead, Jessica tossed the sack at Kirk's face. He grabbed the bag with one hand, shoving Yasmin at Jessica with the other. The two women collided and fell hard, pulling the tethered dog into the pile.

Kirk turned and loped into the undergrowth.

"*Mierda*," Yasmin cursed, untangling herself from Sparky's lead. She tried to stand and fell back to the ground. "Damn it, I've twisted my ankle." She gingerly poked at the rapidly swelling joint. "Damn it all to hell. Jessica could you give me a hand?"

Wiping her mud caked hands on her wet clothes, Jessica reached out and grabbed Yasmin by the elbow. "Okay, put your weight on me." Sparky shook his fur, spraying mud and water in a wide circle around him. "Yeah, thanks pup. I needed that." Growling deep in his throat again, Sparky turned to stare into the dark jungle.

"Who's there?" Jessica demanded, panicked at the thought of Kirk coming back. She gripped Sparky's leash, ready at any moment to let him attack.

"Tranquila, Señorita. May I help?" a Spanish-accented voice asked, as a rain-soaked man dressed in khaki pants and a white shirt stepped into the pathway.

"Who are you?" Fear made Jessica's voice hard and angry.

"I am Javier Cordillo Garcia, an investigator for the INAH, the Instituto Nacional de Antropología e Historia, the National Institute of Anthropology and History." Through the driving rain and battering wind, he held out a plastic-coated identification card in an attempt to prove that he was who he said he was. "I believe that you ladies may have found something that belongs to the people of Mexico."

Slumping in defeat, Jessica uselessly tried to wipe the rain from her face. "Yes, we did, but you are too late." A nearby lightning strike sizzled the air, as another slap of thunder rattled the trees.

"Too late?" he questioned, peering at her through the driving rain.

"Yes, a man, an American, Kirk Patterson, attacked us and stole the few pieces that we'd found."

"Really?" Jessica could hear skepticism in the voice of the man. She watched as he did a cursory check around the pathway, and under the bushes. "Well, we cannot do anything more until this rain stops." He dug out his phone, attempting to take a few photographs of the site. "We will discuss this further in a dryer location, a place more suited to conversation, si?" Pointing at Yasmin's other arm, Cordillo politely asked permission to assist her with walking. "Permítame?"

Yasmin nodded, "Si, gracias."

Wet to the skin and exhausted from the stress of Kirk's unexpected attack, the women slowly made their way down the pathway, shuffling in time to Yasmin's limp. A miserable and wet Sparky trailed behind, still suspicious of the new stranger.

"Señor Cordillo, we came here on a moto. But since Yasmin has injured her ankle, and driving a moto in the rain is difficult, could you help us get to the emergency clinic?" Jessica was hoping that she and Yasmin could have a few minutes to chat in private to get their stories straight. She was also hoping that they could go home and change into dry clothes before being interrogated.

"Si, claro. I have a government car near the side entrance of the park. It will be easier to give you both a ride, even though the hospital is only across the street. I will accompany you." His words were polite and courteous, but Jessica could see the hard edge of his smile. "We can chat there while Señorita Yasmin waits for the doctor."

"Gracias. But, as you can see, I have my dog with me. Is it possible that you could drop us at my house so that I could leave my dog there? Yasmin and I could change into dry clothes before going to the hospital." Fortunately, Jessica had an extra pair of yoga pants and a t-shirt that would fit Yasmin. "We'll also have to call our boss to tell him that we are going to be late for work, and arrange for someone to retrieve Yasmin's moto."

Javier Cordillo smiled inwardly. The blond was a smart one, not cowed by the possibility of arrest, but working every angle she could to her benefit. She obviously didn't want to feel disadvantaged— cold, wet, and dirty—while answering hard questions. Her dark-haired friend was more subdued, probably because of the pain of her injured ankle.

With his background as a former Chief of Detectives in the Mexico City police, he was extremely skeptical of their convenient story of an American man stealing the treasure. He had made a note of the location of the hole where they had been digging. It had been useless to try and take photographs with the camera app on his phone in this foul weather. A full recovery team would have to be dispatched to search for more antiquities. In the meantime, the park would have to be closed and the site guarded.

He pointed at the empty entrance hut. The close proximity of the lightning strikes had probably convinced the attendant that she should lock the main gate and head home as soon as possible. "Wait here while I make a few calls to have the park properly secured. Then I will drive you home before I take you to the hospital." The simple wooden gates at the staff entrance were easy to bypass. They would leave the same way he had entered.

Looking at the wet and dirty dog, and then at the wet and dirty women, Javier sighed to himself. Dog or people, they were all going to mess up the inside of his clean vehicle.

Thumbing a number on his contact list, he watched closely for Jessica's reaction as he said, "You should tell your boss that you won't be at work today. My boss, Jorge Rivera, will have a number of questions for you."

Chapter 31

November 13th Late-morning

Leaving the two women sprawled on the ground in the mud, Kirk had zigged and zagged his way through the woods, hurrying to get to his hotel to pack his few belongings. After that he planned to grab the next passenger boat to the mainland. Usually when the winds were strong, the harbor master would halt the water taxi service between Isla Mujeres and Puerto Juarez, and the last thing he wanted was to be delayed by the storm. Once he was safely in Cancun, he could take a flight anywhere in the world. The bag didn't feel that heavy, but there had to be something inside he could fence for enough money to get him to Cuba, and from there to any country that didn't have an extradition treaty between it and Mexico or the US.

As he hustled past the rain-blurred shape of the pirate Mundaca's house, two large figures separated themselves from the shadows and quickly strode behind him. Roughly grabbing his arms, the men tossed Kirk onto the wet ground, reaching to slap a liquid-soaked gauze pad over his mouth. Kirk's feet slid uselessly in the mud as he battled his attackers. The small cloth bag with the Spanish artifacts tumbled from his hands and disappeared under a nearby bush. Grunting with fury, Kirk attempted to scissor the shorter man's legs out from under his body, but instead kicked the taller one in the testicles.

"Ah, damn it!" the bigger man yelled, his large fist slamming hard into Kirk's left temple, stunning him into unconsciousness. "Son of a bitch. That hurts." He turned sideways, retching up a bit of fluid. Built like an American football linebacker, Diego Avalos was big and tough, and he didn't lose many fights. "He's fast, but thank Christ he's not that strong."

Working quickly, the men secured Kirk's hands and feet with the plastic flex ties used by police to subdue unruly detainees. The damp gauze pad soaked in chloroform was held over Kirk's mouth and nose until they could hear him relax into a deep sleep rhythm. Diego cradled his balls with both hands, attempting to ease the pain. "Oh man, that hurts. No *chucka-chucka* for me this week."

Tempted to make a joke about Diego not needing his testicles anyway, his brother-in-law, Pedro Velazquez, bit down on his sarcastic jibe. "Okay, let's get him loaded." Not nearly as tall as Diego, Pedro had the wide shoulders, long body, and stocky legs of an islander. His ancestry was plainly visible on his handsome face with hooded-deep set eyes, sculpted lips, and a strong blade-shaped nose. When he was a teenager his mother would embarrass him by patting his cheek, telling him he was modeled after the Mayan gods.

They covered Kirk's trussed up hands with a spare t-shirt from Diego's backpack. If anyone happened to notice them, they were hoping they could bluff their way past, saying Kirk had fallen and they were taking him to the hospital for treatment. Half carrying and half dragging an unconscious Kirk, the two men headed towards the park entrance, where they discovered that the large metal gates were closed and locked. Diego pointed in the direction of the staff entrance. It was a simple wooden gate that was seldom locked, allowing the city maintenance workers access to the plant nursery tucked in behind the maintenance shed.

Outside the park, they quickly glanced left and right—no one. No cars, golf carts, or motor-scooters were moving around. There was only rain, wind, and blowing debris on the roads. Everyone was wisely hiding from the storm. "Okay, let's go."

Diego said, limping as quickly as he could towards their plain four-door sedan. As they stuffed Patterson into the trunk, Diego looked over at the white government vehicle sitting next to their car. "Huh. Wonder what the hell Javi is doing here on a nasty day like this?"

"You recognize that car, Diego?" Pedro slammed the trunk lid down, then walked to the driver's side of their vehicle. He made a futile attempt to wipe the rain from his face with his left hand while opening the door with his right. Damn it was wet.

"Yeah, that belongs to Javier Cordillo. He works for some government department. Some kind of investigator or something." He pulled open the passenger door and gingerly slid his aching body into the car.

"Like a cop?" Pedro asked, as he positioned himself behind the steering wheel. *What if a cop had seen them grab the Americano?*

Fiddling with the dashboard controls, Diego tried to clear the moisture from the inside of the windshield, but the humidity from their wet clothes and the heat of their bodies made it an impossible job. "No, not really a cop. More like a government investigator who keeps an eye on antiquities and old stuff that should be in museums. He's an okay guy. I drink beer with him sometimes on Saturdays."

Pedro looked at Diego, skepticism etched on his face. It was one thing to do a favor for a friend, a payback for all of the things he had helped them with, but if they were charged with kidnapping and whatever else, well, he sure as hell wasn't taking the fall all by himself. Carlos better have some juice with these guys. "So, you're sure he's not a real cop?"

"Nah, don't worry. Come on let's get this guy onto the boat and get rid of this trash. It's gonna be a real bitch going out in this storm. Let's just get this job finished."

Chapter 32

November 13th Early afternoon

Three hours later, Yasmin and Jessica slumped dejectedly on hard wooden chairs in the cramped and humid office of Jorge Rivera. Accompanied by the investigator, Javier Cordillo, they had waited at the island community hospital while the doctor examined Yasmin's ankle, pronouncing it sprained, not broken. The doctor had immobilized the joint with an elastic bandage and told her to rest, apply ice, and keep it elevated. Now here they were, being interrogated by two flint-eyed federal officials who were not overly concerned about the rest and ice part of the treatment, but had supplied an additional chair on which she could elevate her damaged limb.

Yasmin was worried. She and Jessica were tucked inside an unremarkable white building near Centro. No one, not even Carlos, knew where they were. It was the type of building that anyone would pass by without even wondering who worked inside—plain, unassuming, and with no identifying signage. Their fun and silly adventure had just turned serious.

The boss, Jorge Rivera, finally spoke just as Yasmin started to fidget under his scrutiny. "Señorita Medina, how exactly did you find this treasure?"

She was exhausted from waiting, sitting, and wondering how much trouble they were in. Her ankle throbbed, her head hurt, and she was dying of thirst. "I already explained that in great detail to your investigator, Señor Cordillo," she replied, politely but with a sharp edge to her voice.

"Si, claro. But you must now explain it to me, in great detail." His scrutiny centered on her eyes.

Sighing wearily again, Yasmin said. "We found a letter from Fermin Mundaca to La Trigueña, explaining that he had located the treasure and then he had moved it." Yasmin stifled a yawn with her right hand. "May we please have a drink of water? It has been a very long day and we are very tired."

"Of course." Rivera indicated to Javier Cordillo to get both women a bottle of water from the cupboard behind his chair. He waited until the bottles had been opened and quickly consumed by the women before resuming his questioning. "So, you said you found a letter. Where exactly?"

This was the tricky part, Yasmin knew, as she and Jessica had decided not to admit to stealing the flask, with the letter inside, from the graveyard in Centro. "It was in with a bunch of papers that my grandmother asked me to sort out." *I'm going to hell for sure, for lying and for including mis abuela in my lies.*

"I see. How did your grandmother obtain this letter?" Rivera met her gaze before giving her a look that conveyed he didn't believe her.

"My grandmother is convinced we are descended from La Trigueña and that I look like her," she said, pointing at her green eyes and then indicating her curly dark hair that was streaked with blond highlights. "Perhaps the letter was handed down to her by her ancestors, but she didn't know what it was..." Yasmin's voice trailed off. Even she could hear the lies in her words.

"I see," Rivera repeated, shifting his attention towards Jessica. "And you, Miss, em, Sanderson, do you agree with what Señorita Medina has said?"

"Yes." Jessica straightened up, meeting his intimidating stare. "Yes, I do. We meant no harm, we just thought it would be a lark to search for treasure."

"Pardon me, Miss Sanderson. I don't understand what you mean by 'a *lark*'." His face crunched in puzzlement. "What does this mean?"

"An adventure." She smiled, warming to her fabrication, "You know, pirates, damsels in distress, all that fun stuff." Jessica pretended to wave a blade through the air, imitating a sword fight. "It was like being a little kid again, imagining what we would do with all that gold. It was all just a silly fantasy. We meant no harm."

"And *what* would you have done with all of that gold, Miss Sanderson?"

"We would have reported it immediately, had we not been caught in the storm, and then attacked by that knife-wielding maniac Kirk Patterson."

Trying not to laugh at the audacity of the young women, Rivera sliced a can-you-believe-this glance at his subordinate. Cordillo curbed a grin and looked away. Rivera had to admit that the women were coming up with a really inventive story. *Pirates and damsels in distress. Hilarious.*

The INAH, the Instituto Nacional de Antropología e Historia, only had a small presence on the island to protect the federally owned

Hacienda Mundaca Estate Park, located mid-island. The cost of keeping the office open was a source of irritation to the federal government bean counters. There were only two employees, himself, plus Javi who worked part-time as an investigator, but it was a yearly struggle to maintain a federal presence on the island.

Jorge settled back in his chair, assuming a more conciliatory posture. There was still something the women weren't telling him, but he was delighted that he had accidentally overheard the two Americanos discussing the Spanish coin during his lunch break the day before. It was funny how one thing led to another and here he was—at the center of a big discovery. Having foiled an attempted theft of a valuable national treasure, it was possible that both he and Javier would be considered heroes. Well, not exactly foiled the robbery, as hypothetically the Americano did make off with the coins that the women had dug up. But there was bound to be a lot more loot according to the information the women had given Javier. Captain Lorencillo de Graaf had apparently buried the bulk of his treasure on Isla Mujeres. Anticipating the media attention, this could be his ticket to a promotion, a move to a larger city, perhaps even to Mexico City. He had to handle this situation just right to impress the head office bosses.

Scribbling a few sentences in his notebook, Rivera let the silence stretch, hoping one of the women would start babbling nervously, revealing the information they were holding back. Silence was a time-proven trick used by investigators and interrogators as guilty people felt the need to fill the silence with words, words that eventually would dig them deeper into trouble. Strangely enough neither woman took the bait, remaining silent until he himself spoke first. "All right then. That's all for this evening. We will investigate your discovery tomorrow, once the storm has passed. It is now a named storm, Tropical Storm Ricardo, but it is forecast to move quickly across the island."

"Señorita Medina, please do not leave the island. Miss Sanderson, you will bring me your passport tomorrow at nine in the morning." Rivera put on his meanest bad-cop face and glared at Jessica. "You will not leave the island and not leave Mexico until we get this straightened out. Are we clear?"

Jessica dipped her head, chastened. "Yes, I understand perfectly. I will be here at nine tomorrow morning with my passport. Should I also bring a lawyer?"

Chapter 33

November 13th Early evening

Driving cautiously along the storm flooded streets, an unsmiling Javier Cordillo dropped the two women at Jessica's colorfully painted house, nodding curtly at their whispered thank-yous. It was late, but his boss had decided that Javier should park somewhere close by on the street and keep an eye on the women. Jorge thought there might be a chance that Kirk Patterson would return to threaten them. Javi didn't mind the unpaid overtime. It was slightly more interesting than sitting at home alone, drinking beer, and watching some brainless TV program again.

The women had decided that since Yasmin needed assistance getting dressed and undressed, plus Sparky would have to be let out to do his business, it was easier to stay together at Jessica's place rather than relocate to Yasmin's. Cordillo had stopped briefly at Yasmin's house, checking it carefully for intruders before allowing the women to gather up toiletries and a change of clothing. Then he drove them to Jessica's a short distance away, again checking the inside for intruders or signs of an attempted break-in. Parking his nondescript car amongst the neighborhood collection of old *motos* and battered vehicles, Javier rested comfortably against the driver's door. He was fairly certain the women thought he had gone home for the night. The heavy rain made it difficult to see through his windshield, but so far, everything was quiet at the house.

"We have well and truly landed in the doo-doo," huffed Jessica, as she helped Yasmin over to the sofa. "Surrendering my passport tomorrow is a frightening thought."

"We'll figure this out, Jessica. We can ask Luis Aguilar, the local *Notario*, to help us. He's a friend of Carlos." Yasmin gratefully stretched out on the small navy-blue sofa, arranging the brightly colored throw-pillows into a pile to keep her ankle elevated. "I'm exhausted. Do you think we should call Carlos tonight and apologize? Or leave it until morning?"

"Oh hell. When I told him we wouldn't be at work today, I admitted we had been detained by INAH. I also mentioned that we'd had a run in with

Kirk, but I didn't give him the details. He'll be worried." Jessica picked up her iPhone and turned it back on. The flood of missed calls and messages from Carlos pinged rapidly into the phone. "Oh, yeah. He's worried." She punched his name on her contact list, listening until he answered. "Yep, hi Carlos. It's me, Jessica. Whoa, whoa. We're home and okay. At my house." She looked at Yasmin, continuing to listen to his barrage of questions. "Yes, sure, please come by." She watched as Yasmin nodded in agreement. "It's easier to explain in person. Okay, see you soon."

Preparing to disconnect the call, she heard another question. "What? Food? Sure, we are starving, and thirsty if you happen to have a few beers that you could bring as well. Great, thank you so much."

Too tired to stand, Jessica slumped into a comfortable chair, dejectedly looking at her friend. "Okay he should be here soon. Do you want anything in the meantime? Pain killer? Ice for your foot? Anything?"

Yasmin swiped a damp curl away from her eyes; then her hand drifted to the bandage on her throat, "I would really like to start this day over." She paused and searched out her friend's gaze. "Kirk terrified me."

"Yeah, me too. Me too."

"What do we tell Carlos?"

"Everything, Yasmin. We are in over our heads on this."

Twenty minutes later a loud rap on the wooden front door startled Jessica. She had dozed off curled in the chair. "That's probably Carlos." She heaved herself to her feet and walked to the door. As she twisted the door handle a strong blast of wind, a remnant of the fast-moving Tropical Storm Ricardo, slapped it wide open.

"Why didn't you have your security chain on the door?" Carlos demanded, ducking inside. He reached out and helped Jessica push the door closed against the angry wind. Politely slipping off his wet sandals, he stood dripping onto an absorbent door mat.

"What? Oh. We were too tired to care, and besides Sparky is a good alarm system." She pointed at the dog, standing by her feet.

"Really. Then why didn't he bark when I knocked?" Carlos snapped at Jessica.

Jessica tiredly regarded her boss as she handed him a towel to dry his hair and face. "He knows you Carlos. He's met you before." Was he going to give her grief all night, or would he listen to their story?

"Yeah, well, okay. But you should still use the security chain." He handed the take-out Styrofoam containers to Jessica, then stepping carefully on the wet tile floor, he placed a plastic bag with a six-pack of Sol beers on her kitchen counter. "I had the restaurant kitchen make up two orders of fish and chips for you." Cracking the top of one beer he handed it to Jessica, then opened a second one and took it over to Yasmin. "How's the foot?" he asked, his voice softer, eyes searching her face. Then, as he noticed the bandage under her chin, his eyebrows shot up. "What happened to your throat?"

"Just a scratch," she said self-consciously, holding her right hand over the bandage. "It's fine, thank you. My ankle is a bit swollen, but it will be fine in a day or two." She smiled tightly at him, "No stilettos for me for a week or two, I'm afraid. That's going to absolutely kill my tips."

"Jesus, Yasmin. This isn't a game." Carlos ran his hand through his thick black hair, frustration etching his face.

"I know, I know. This whole thing started out as a joke."

"Tell me. Please, tell me everything so I can help."

Uncertain, Yasmin looked at Jessica, who nodded. "Yes, everything. This is more than we can handle."

Yasmin regarded the half-empty bottle of beer in her hand. Holding it up she said, "Well it is going to take more than just a beer for me to tell this story. Any chance you have a glass of wine somewhere in this house?"

Chapter 34

November 13th Late night

Close to midnight Carlos leaned back in the chair. He had been tensely perched on the edge of the seat while he listened to the long story, starting with the women drunkenly defiling the empty grave of the Pirate Mundaca, all the way up to today's rain-soaked fiasco at the park and their long, tense interview with the INAH officials.

"Jesus. This sounds like a plot for a Johnny Depp *Pirates of the Caribbean* movie." Carlos muttered, shaking his head in disbelief. He leaned forward, and sat with his elbows on his knees, wondering how much to tell the women about Patterson. If he told them about Kirk being wanted in Florida as a suspected killer who drugged his victims with roofies, it could make them more fearful for their own safety. If he didn't tell them about Kirk/Kyle's history, and they found out later, would either of them trust him again? And he sure as hell couldn't tell them what he had asked Diego and Pedro to do with Kirk without tipping his hand. That was a secret best kept just between the three friends.

Jessica's face creased in a tired grin, "This has been one hell of an adventure, starting when we borrowed the map from Mundaca's crypt."

"Borrowed!" Yasmin uncontrollably snorted a laugh. "Yeah, we borrowed it alright."

Carlos looked from Yasmin to Jessica, perplexed. *What the hell are they talking about now?*

Wheezing with suppressed laughter, Jessica tried to explain to Carlos her granddad's mining-community theory of borrowing as opposed to stealing. "As long as we return it, it's not stolen. Just borrowed." She guffawed, tears running down her face as she giggled hysterically. "Honestly, we planned to return the map just as soon as we found the treasure."

Yasmin joined in the hilarity, holding her ribs as the gales of laughter escaped. "Ow, ow, ow. My foot," she sputtered, as her sprained ankle threatened to slide off the precarious pile of small cushions. Steadying her leg with both hands, she added, "I am sore and tired and damn mad, but, God, this feels good to laugh. It makes me feel alive and strong."

Wiping her eyes with a piece of paper towel torn from a roll on the kitchen counter, Jessica finally got her giggles under control. "It's been one hell of a day."

"*Saludos hermana!*" Yasmin sputtered, then downed the last sip of wine in an ironic salute to their escapade.

Carlos forced a grin. He was glad they still had a sense of humor after their ordeal. "Alright then ladies, it's late." He reached out to take the empty wine glass from Yasmin's hand, her fingers lightly grazing his. A spark sizzled through his fingertips, burning a pathway along his nerve endings, squeezing his heart with emotion. "Why don't I spend the night on the sofa?" he asked softly.

"No, truly we'll be fine. We have Sparky as our security system." She smiled up at him, "Tomorrow will be a long day, and we all need to get a decent sleep."

Nodding his understanding, he didn't force the issue. Diego had called earlier in the afternoon to say the 'package' was safely secured in their cruiser. Still, he felt a little deflated that Yasmin didn't want him to stay. "You have to be at the INAH at nine in the morning." He pocketed his phone and picked up his car keys. "I'll contact Luis Aguilar about your run-in with the government officials. We'll meet you tomorrow outside their office before Jessica hands in her passport."

"Gracias, Carlos. How can we ever thank you?" Yasmin stifled a yawn, as she waved goodbye from the sofa.

"De nada, don't worry, it is nothing. Just no more adventures—at least until we get this mess sorted out." At the front door, he pointed to the security chain. "Keep that on, please."

Jessica followed Carlos to the entrance, waving goodbye. As she turned to relock the door, she glanced down the street. Weird. There was a white four-door, plain-Jane car parked three spaces down from her house. It looked similar to the white sedan that the INAH guy, Javier Cordillo, drove when he brought them home. Stepping back inside, Jessica slid the security chain into the slot. It wasn't much of a deterrent, but at least it provided a little more protection. If that guy Javier was watching their house, it couldn't hurt to have another pair of eyes on them. It wasn't like she and Yasmin were going to sneak off in the middle of the night and dig for more treasure. The tropical storm still fretted overhead. One minute it was pouring rain, the next the rain stopped. Then the wind gusted and rattled the single-pane glass in her windows and pushed against her thin door. It felt like an intruder forcing his way inside.

Tomorrow, they would face the consequences of their actions. *Oh, joy*.

Chapter 35

November 14th Early morning

By dawn of the next day, Tropical Storm Ricardo had expended its energy, downgrading to remnants of a tropical depression moving further west into the mainland of Mexico. Many of the low-lying streets on Isla Mujeres were flooded, especially at the intersections where the runoff from the hilly areas emptied into the lower streets and eventually flowed into the ocean. Drivers cautiously made their way around broken tree branches and rubbish littering the streets. Many storm drains were blocked with an accumulation of leaves or plastic bags, preventing the removal of the excess water. The rising sun brought higher temperatures and increased humidity, making the air sticky and hot. Three days from now a new population of mosquitoes would hatch out, hungry and looking to feast on the island residents.

At the Hacienda Mundaca Park, a soggy figure shuffled under the low-lying vegetation. Dizzy and unable to stand after slamming headfirst into a large rock, Ryan had weathered the storm huddled under a bush. His left knee was swollen and sore. He needed help to walk but the park was quiet and empty; there was no one within shouting distance. Licking his dry lips, he thought how ironic it was that he was thirsty, after being pounded all night by a storm. He'd tried to capture some of the rain by tipping his head back, but at times it was raining so hard he was afraid of drowning. Whatever had happened last night, he hoped that he had seen the last of Kirk Patterson, that nasty son-of-a-bitch. Unfortunately, no one else but Kirk knew he was in the park, and he really did need help. *Christ what a mess.*

As the sun rose higher, the temperature kept pace. Seemingly hours later, Ryan could hear a group of people walking up the pathway. The clinking of metal sounded like they were carrying tools. Maybe they were park employees checking on storm damage? Ryan gingerly scooted on his haunches closer to the pathway. "Hola. Hola. I need help," he croaked through his dry throat. "Help. Please help me!"

A worried female face appeared around a corner in the pathway, "What's happened?" she asked Ryan, as a crowd of laborers pressed in close behind her, craning their necks for a better view of his wet mud-caked form sitting at the edge of the trail.

Ryan indicated his head and his knee. "I'm hurt. I need help."

The woman pulled a fresh bottle of water from her backpack and offered it to Ryan. Speaking in fluent English, she said that her name was Sarah Ordoñez, and she worked for the Cancun division of the INAH, the Instituto Nacional de Antropología e Historia. She pulled a small first aid kit from her pack, removing a gauze pad and handing it to Ryan. "Here, your head is still bleeding a bit. Press this pad on the wound. I'll call for assistance for you."

"Thank you, so much." Ryan tilted his head, pressing the gauze pad gently against his head wound. "What are you doing here?" Hoping he could bluff his way out of an awkward situation, he kept what he assumed was an interested and innocent expression on his face.

"I could ask the same of you, Señor." Her dark eyes steadily observed him, a faint smile flickering across her lips as she pulled her phone from her back pocket and skimmed through her contact list.

"I was exploring the park and fell." He smiled feebly, playing up his helplessness. "I couldn't walk so I spent the night here."

"Yes, of course. Exploring the park," she said, her expression neutral. "Momentito," she said, pinching her thumb and forefinger into a semi-circle, the local sign for *give me just a moment*.

Ryan studied the woman's face as she thumbed the buttons on her phone, then spoke to someone called Jorge. "*Si, un otro Americano.*" She nodded at a reply that Ryan couldn't hear, then answered. "He needs medical attention. He has a head wound and an injured leg. Will you arrange for the ambulance crew to assist him to the hospital? Yes, yes. I'll stay with him. The rest of the crew can proceed with their assignment. *Si, claro. Gracias.*"

As she disconnected the call, Ryan's eyes tracked Sarah as she walked towards one of the waiting crew members. "Juan José, please take over for me. The site should be a little further up the pathway where the cave is located. Hopefully, you will see signs of the ground being disturbed, although the storm may have erased any marks. If you find a likely spot, start the excavation, but be careful with those shovels." Pointing at the camera hanging on a wide strap from Juan José's shoulder, she added, "And remember to take photos, lots of photos. We don't want to be accused of any improprieties." Curiosity etched on their faces, the workers carefully stepped around Ryan's outstretched injured leg, murmuring "*Con permiso,*" politely as they passed by.

Sarah flicked a cool smile at Ryan. "I will wait with you until medical assistance arrives. The hospital is a short distance away. It is just across the street from the park entrance. The local supervisor for INAH, Jorge Rivera, and his investigator, Javier Cordillo, will meet you at the hospital. Señor Rivera wishes to speak with you about your mishap."

"Me?" Ryan's voice squeaked. "He wants to talk to me? Why?"

Sarah shrugged. "It is just a formality. We have had a report of illegal treasure hunting in the park. This park is protected federal property." She nonchalantly shrugged again. "We are simply interviewing all potential witnesses."

"But," sputtered Ryan, "I don't understand. I was injured. Not treasure hunting."

"Yes, of course. Don't worry, Señor. I am certain it is just a formality."

Chapter 36

November 14th Mid-morning

Yasmin waved a hand at a distant taxi, indicating they wanted a ride. Her arm slung around Jessica's shoulders, she hobbled to the curb, waiting for the battered red Nissan Tsuru to stop.

Sliding awkwardly across the seat of the taxi, Yasmin kept her injured leg stuck straight out, taking up most of the room in the back. Jessica closed the door for Yasmin, then hopped into the front seat. "The INAH office in Centro, please," requested Yasmin.

"Where?"

Yasmin described in detail the building and the nearby businesses.

Finally, the driver nodded. "Okay, now I know where you mean."

Leaning back on the seat, Yasmin tried to ignore the pain in her foot and ankle. At least nothing was broken, but it was still going to be difficult to work with a useless leg. Carlos was being unbelievably understanding about the hours at the bar that she and Jessica were missing. The rest of the staff were probably not happy, working extra hours to cover their shifts. She and Jessica would have a lot of fence mending to do when they returned to the *Loco Lobo* if, and it was a big if, they still had their freedom at the end of the week.

Gazing at the storm damage through the window, Jessica grumbled. "We still have to get you a pair of crutches today. I don't understand why the hospital doesn't keep a bunch on hand to rent out or to sell."

"They just don't," Yasmin replied tartly. "Patients have to find their own, somewhere." Occasionally even Jessica could annoy her with her assumptions that Canadian or American practices were superior to the everyday routines in Mexico. *You are in a different country. It is what it is; get over it.*

"Okay, okay. I'm sorry, I'm sorry." Jessica replied contritely.

"Sure, no worries." Yasmin answered, thinking, *I'm sorry,* Jessica usually said that at least a dozen times a day. Automatic uttering of the expression seemed to be a prerequisite for all

Canadians to retain their citizenship. Just one of the funny little differences between their two cultures.

Turning in the seat to whisper to Yasmin, Jessica said, "Assuming everything goes well today, I'll check at the various pharmacies for crutches." Then a mischievous grin played across her face as she spoke in a normal voice. "But since you are incapacitated, I'll need to drive your pretty little moto-bike, so that I can search properly."

Yasmin sputtered, "Drive my new bike? I don't think so."

"Ha, you're just too easy to get riled up about your shiny new toy," Jessica said with a strained laugh.

Yasmin smiled in acknowledgement at Jessica's attempt to lighten their somber mood. She reached over the back of the seat and squeezed her shoulder. "We'll be okay. Really, I have faith in Carlos and Luis."

Stopping at the plain white building Yasmin had described, the taxi driver reached his hand back over his shoulder as Yasmin deposited the fare in his outstretched palm. With a murmured "*Gracias*," she slid out of the taxi. Leaning on the door frame while she sorted herself out, she gingerly put her foot down on the paving stones. She met Jessica's worried look and winked. "Okay, chica, let's do this."

Leaning on Jessica and hopping towards the door, she was thankful that Jorge Rivera's office was on the main floor of the building, otherwise she would have had to climb the stairs one at a time like a toddler.

Jessica pulled open the unmarked door, and she and Yasmin stepped into the tiny, stuffy foyer to find Carlos already there. Luis Aguilar leaned against a wall, waiting patiently.

Carlos clutched a new pair of aluminum crutches in his right hand. "Hola, Yasmin. I got these for you," he said pointing at the crutches. "If we need to change the length it's an easy adjustment." He flicked a sideways glance at Luis, catching an amused twitch of a smile on his friend's face.

"They're perfect Carlos," she responded warmly. "You've saved the day, again."

Luis stuffed down his laughter as an image of Carlos as a bashful knight-in-shining-amour flashed through his brain.

Yasmin extended her right hand in greeting. "Buenos Dias, Luis. Thank you so much for coming." Indicating Jessica, she added, "This is my friend, Jessica Sanderson."

Aguilar gently reached out and lightly grasped the fingertips of Jessica's right hand in the abbreviated softer touch of a Latino who would normally kiss an acquaintance on the cheek, not shake hands. "Mucho gusto, Señorita Jessica," he said, appraising the slim blue-eyed blond.

"Gracias, Señor Aguilar. It's a pleasure to meet you as well." Jessica politely bobbed her head. "I've been told I have to surrender my passport today. That terrifies me."

"Please, call me Luis. When you call me Señor Aguilar, it makes me feel old, very old." Turning to smile at Yasmin, he continued. "I believe you were trying for a realistic experience, as part of your research for your treasure hunting novel. Correct?" He nodded his head up and down in an exaggerated motion, meaning *Just agree with what I said*.

"Yes of course." Yasmin readily agreed. "That's exactly what we were doing, research for my novel."

"Perfecto. No harm in that." He pointed at the interior office door. "Now let's go talk to these gentlemen."

An hour later, the foursome exited the INAH building. "That went well," Luis said, beaming in satisfaction at the others. "A little lawyer-ese, a few big words, lots of references to Yasmin's embryonic career as an author, and Señorita Jessica's passport problem is resolved." He brushed his hands together, dusting away the problem. "However, we still have an illegal treasure hunting charge that might take a little more work to fix. Our meeting tomorrow with the officials from the Cancun office is going to take a bit more finesse."

Chapter 37

November 14th Late-morning

Luis strode into his compact and thankfully air-conditioned office, smiling amicably at his assistant. "Yolanda, you may have the rest of the day off. I'm just going to tidy up a few documents and then leave early myself." In the small two-person office, he expected her to work the same long hours that he did, and a half-day off would be an unexpected bonus for Yolanda.

Yolanda Rincale's eyebrows popped up in surprise. "Really, Señor Aguilar? A half-day off?"

"Si, si, with pay of course. I just need a little personal time today." He made a shooing motion with his hands, wanting her to be out of the office before the others arrived. Yolanda was a dedicated employee, but he didn't want her to be involved, or she might be forced to lie for him at a later date. It was simpler this way. He had a brilliant new strategy for defending Yasmin and Jessica against the possible unlawful treasure hunting accusation.

"Gracias," Yolanda said, as she quickly powered off her computer and gathered up her purse and mobile phone. "I appreciate the extra time, Señor Aguilar. I have been neglecting my household chores recently, and this is a good opportunity for me to catch up." She stopped and turned to look at Luis before exiting the office. "Tomorrow morning at the normal time?"

"Si, Yolanda, eight in the morning." He waved goodbye, "See you tomorrow," as he shut the front door and flipped the sign over to "Closed." Rubbing his hands together, he considered his game plan. The little story about Yasmin being an aspiring novelist, who was merely conducting realistic research for her novel, worked to a point. Jorge Rivera and his investigator Javi had skeptically listened to his long tale of bullshit. They weren't fully convinced, but since their employer, Carlos, vouched for both women, they had decided to let Jessica keep her passport, for now.

As for the illegal treasure hunting problem, well that was going to take a bit more creativity. Luis pulled out a fresh pad of paper, quickly scratching handwritten notes as his fertile mind spun through the possibilities. Yasmin's grandmother truly believed she was a descendent of La Trigueña, the object of affection for Pirate Mundaca. So, it stood to reason that Señora Maria Guadalupe Medina thought she was entitled to the treasure.

Nodding in self-agreement to his fabrication, Luis continued scribbling notes. Señora Medina had probably inadvertently encouraged Yasmin to go on this little escapade with her oral legends of unrequited love, lost treasure, family history, and so on and so on. Yasmin, being an impressionable young child when she first heard the stories, was convinced that her grandmother was the legal owner of the treasure. He chuckled lightly—*yeah, good one.* This just might work. Blame it on the old woman influencing a young kid. With a flick of his wrist, he tossed his pen and the pad on his desk. *Perfecto. Luis, you are a star.*

Sipping from a bottle of cold water, Luis leaned back comfortably in his office chair, waiting for the others to arrive. Calmly reflecting on the strange events centering on Yasmin and Jessica, he briefly wondered what had happened to that guy, Kirk Patterson. After attacking the women at the Hacienda Mundaca Park and snatching the bag of whatever treasure they had located, he had simply disappeared. Strange. *I wonder if he is holed up somewhere on the island, or did he manage to board the passenger ferry for Cancun before the authorities were alerted?*

A light rap on the window signalled the group had arrived. Luis enthusiastically hopped out of his chair and unlocked the door, swinging it open. "Come in, come in." He motioned for Carlos, Jessica and Yasmin to enter. Luis stuck his head out the door, glancing furtively from side to side, as if he was afraid that someone was spying on their meeting. Seeing nothing that worried him, he moved back inside and relocked the door.

Carlos chuckled at Luis' comical antics, "Jesus, Luis, you look really guilty behaving like that."

He shrugged his shoulders. "Just paranoia—goes with the job I guess." Indicating the two client chairs in front of his desk, Luis said, "Sit down, please." He pulled Yolanda's computer chair over for Carlos to use. "All right then. Here's my plan." He quickly briefed the group on his ideas, adding, "Yasmin, we will need to include your grandmother as a witness for you."

"No! She knows nothing about this. Leave her out of it," Yasmin exclaimed.

"Yasmin, think about it. Please." Luis made calming motions with his hands. "She is the perfect person to tell the INAH officials that you meant no harm. You were merely investigating your family's oral history." Luis smiled reassuringly. "This is a very serious charge that they are contemplating against you and Miss Sanderson. Trust me on this, please."

Yasmin's green eyes sought out Carlos. "She will be so ashamed of me," she whispered, dropping her gaze into her lap.

Carlos opened his mouth to disagree, but Jessica cut in before he could say a word. "Ashamed of you? Yasmin, give the woman some credit. I've met your grandmother. If you'd told her what we were up to she would have joined us for the adventure." Jessica leaned forward to press her point, staring intently at Yasmin. "Your grandmother is a powerhouse, tough as nails, and drop-dead gorgeous. She'll knock those stuffy INAH *jefes* on their asses."

Intrigued, Luis cocked an eyebrow at Carlos, silently asking, *is this true?*

Carlos just shrugged, his palms out, indicating that he had no clue about Señora Medina's personality.

"Yasmin?" Luis questioned. "May I please have your grandmother's telephone number and address?"

"Alright," Yasmin said, as she slowly wrote the information on a piece of paper. "I know she's home. I spoke with her earlier." She held the paper close to her chest for a moment, then handed it to Luis. "I just needed to hear her voice, but she doesn't know what I've done."

"*Bien*. Leave it with me. I will catch the next passenger ferry. I have a car in the Puerto Juarez parking lot, and I can be in Valladolid in a couple of hours. It is better for me to discuss this with her in person." Luis gathered up his notes, unwilling to leave them lying around for Yolanda to stumble upon.

"Alright then, I'll contact you all when I am back on the island. We have a meeting with the INAH officials scheduled for tomorrow at ten in the morning. We'll need to be well prepared."

Chapter 38

November 15th Mid-morning

Thumping through the ocean swell in the Gulf of Mexico, the fifty-eight-foot Viking, the *Bruja del Mar* (Sea Witch), was making good time. Her twin twelve-hundred-horse MAN diesels were running sweet and steady. Diego Avalos stood spread-legged behind the wheel, balanced on the balls of his feet, knees flexed to absorb the motion as the big craft lifted and dropped on the waves. Co-owners of a sport-fishing charter business, he and his brother-in-law Pedro Velázquez were both expert seamen. They shared the piloting duties as their older but well-maintained yacht pounded north through the swells.

The remnants of Tropical Storm Ricardo had veered inland through central Mexico away from the Gulf. The sun glinted off the mint green water and a pod of playful dolphins swam powerfully through the bow wave, pacing the fast, white boat.

Flicking on the cabin intercom, Diego called to Pedro. "Hey bud, it's coming up to your watch. I'm beat. I need a break."

"I'm up. Just give me ten minutes to make a fresh pot of coffee."

Fifteen minutes later, Pedro climbed up to the upper steering station. "Here you go, brain food. Two sugars, and milk." He offered Diego a cup of strong, hot coffee, and then scanned the Satnav and radar, checking their route and location.

"Ahhh! I needed this." Diego gratefully slurped a mouthful of the fortifying brew. "How's our guest doing?" He flicked his head, indicating the back deck.

Pedro flashed a wry smile, "About as good as can be expected, I guess. He's pissed his pants and stinks like a pig." Pedro shrugged his shoulders, running his hand over his shaved head in a familiar gesture. "Not too good for the mahogany decking, but it'll rinse off once were done."

"Just a few more hours and we'll be rid of him." Diego stretched his back muscles, bending backwards and sideways. "I'm beat. You okay for the next four hours?"

"Of course. Check on that *pendejo* when you come back. We wouldn't want him to die too soon." Pedro settled into a comfortable position, relaxed and confident. He'd done this trip on the Sea Witch a number of times. She was seaworthy, strong and well-balanced. The weather was perfect, but the trip was still long and tiring. He made a slight course correction, then flicked on the autopilot. Nothing to do but watch for obstructions and enjoy the ride. As he settled into the rhythm of the boat, Pedro contemplated their current task for Carlos. Soon they would be rid of this piece of human garbage. Hopefully that INAH cop, Javi Cordillo, hadn't seen them at the park when they snatched Patterson. Fingering his satellite phone, Pedro debated about calling with an update. Unsure if his call could be tracked or monitored by some faceless government agency, he decided it was worth the risk. The tone purred in his ear four times before Carlos' rich voice answered.

"Si, Bueno?"

"Hola," Pedro answered, purposely not greeting his friend by name, and not identifying himself. His eyes flicked repeatedly to the water ahead, the Satnav, the radar, gauges and around again, checking for potential problems.

"Where are you?"

"Boating." He paused, hoping that Carlos would get the idea that he wanted to be circumspect with details.

"Yes, of course. Everything okay?"

Slurping a large mouthful of coffee, Pedro swallowed before answering, "Si, the weather is perfect. We'll deliver the package later this evening." Pedro quickly scanned the radar for other marine traffic before returning his attention to the phone conversation. "Everything okay with you?"

"A few minor details that had to be cleared up. Nothing important," replied Carlos.

Pedro tensed, gripping the phone tighter. "Anything we should be concerned about?" His eyes rapidly scanned his surroundings for US Coast Guard cruisers and spotter planes. *Jesus, calm down. Don't act guilty like a smuggler.*

"No, no. Don't worry. It was just a small problem concerning one of my employees," Carlos answered evasively, certain that Pedro would understand that he meant Yasmin. "We'll have it sorted soon."

"Okay then. Call me later if anything comes up that we should know about." He hoped that wasn't too blatant a hint if their call was being monitored.

"Si, claro. Have a good day on the water. Maybe you should do a little chumming for shark," Carlos added with a dry laugh.

"Good idea. See you soon, my friend." Pedro disconnected the call, settling the phone into its storage slot. His eyes never stopped roaming the ocean surface checking for debris and driftwood. They were still a long way from their destination, and if they dinged the prop on the boat it would seriously slow down their timetable.

Four hours later, refreshed from a short nap and a hot shower, Diego ambled out of the below-deck stateroom, headed to the back deck. He kicked at the trussed-up form laying in the shade of the overhang. "Hey, *pendejo*, you still alive? Whew, you smell like you're already dead." He waved his hand in front of his face, fanning away the rank smell of urine.

A muffled grunt was the only response.

"Oh, right. I guess you can't talk with duct tape over your mouth. Here, let me fix that for you." With one quick snap of his wrist, Diego yanked the tape from Kirk's mouth, tearing the thin skin from his lips.

"Shit!" Kirk yelled, thrashing on the wooden deck, straining against his bonds. "You're a dead man!"

"Oh. Did that hurt?" Diego's dark eyes stared flatly at their captive. This scumbag was a waste of space in an overcrowded world. "Listen, *pendejo*, this is your one chance. Do you want water? Or should I just let you die of thirst? It would save time if you did."

"Let me go. I'll make it worth your while." Kirk writhed on the deck, pulling against his restraints. "I've got money. Lots of money." He spat, rage glowing in his eyes. His pupils were so large and so black Diego could have sworn he was looking into the soulless eyes of a Great White shark.

Keeping his eyes pinned on Patterson, Diego turned his head slightly to yell over his shoulder, "Hey, Pedro, did you hear that? He says he'll pay us to let him go. What do you think?"

Snorting a derisive laugh, Pedro answered, "Sure. Ten million American dollars each would about cover it. Does that work for you, Diego?"

"Only ten million?" Diego pretended to mull it over, then shook his head. "Naw, I'd need about twenty million to keep me in style with beautiful señoritas, cold cervezas, and tacos for the rest of my life." He reached for the roll of duct tape and ripped off a length. Dropping one knee onto Kirk's chest to keep him pinned to the deck, Diego tightly reapplied the sticky tape.

"I guess you didn't want a drink of water."

Chapter 39

November 15th Mid-morning

The following morning, Yasmin slowly maneuvered with her crutches into the main entrance at the Municipal Hall, pausing at the double glass doors as Luis Aguilar held one open for her. Carlos and Jessica trailed behind. The Cancun INAH officials had scheduled a preliminary hearing to decide if they were going to press charges for illegal treasure hunting.

At ten minutes to ten, a tall and very elegant woman strode into the conference room, heading directly towards Yasmin. "Yasmin, mi amor, how are you?" Señora Maria Guadalupe Medina awkwardly wrapped her arms around her granddaughter and the crutches. "You should have called me immediately." Turning to Jessica, the woman gave her a warm hug, adding, "Jessica, so nice to see you again."

"Abuela, I apologize for causing this problem," Yasmin uttered as she gazed at her grandmother. She was sixty-nine years old, but she could easily pass for mid-fifties. Turning to her group of friends, Yasmin indicated Luis and Carlos. "*Abuela*, you have already met Señor Aguilar, and this is my boss and close friend, Señor Carlos Mendoza."

Carlos extended his hand and gently took the older woman's hand in his. "Enchanted," he said, smiling warmly.

"Gracias, Señor Mendoza." Maria dipped her head politely in acknowledgement of his compliment. "Now, Señor Aguilar, yesterday we discussed your strategy for this meeting, and I think it is a very good plan. I can be very convincing." She smiled wryly at the group as she pulled an intricately embroidered shawl and a lacy fan from her bag. "I am just a silly old woman who filled her impressionable young granddaughter's head with fanciful tales of pirates, treasure, and unreciprocated love for a beautiful young woman." Draping the shawl over her head and shoulders, she fanned herself demurely, instantly transforming into a mild-mannered elderly woman who was terribly distraught over her granddaughter's legal problem.

Yasmin swallowed a chuckle as the door to the conference room swung open and two very serious-faced men and one woman entered the room. This group held her fate in their hands. It would not be helpful if the officials thought that she was laughing at them, when in reality she was amused by how quickly her grandmother could change her appearance with just a bit of cloth and a fan.

Walking briskly towards the conference room table, a round-faced pudgy man addressed the group. "Good morning everyone. Please be seated," he said waving to chairs placed around the long table. "I am César Avila Barbosa, the General Manager for the Cancun office of the Instituto Nacional de Antropología e Historia. He then proceeded to introduce the other committee members in a blur of long and complicated formal names.

Settling into a chair, the chairman pointed at Jorge Rivera who had just entered the room, "Señor Rivera, would you please start the proceedings with your report."

Rivera nodded and stood with his hands resting on the back of a chair. He began to recount the events as he knew them, from the tampering with Mundaca's empty grave to the discovery of the treasure.

"Your honor," Luis Aguilar interjected, "this is all second-hand information told to Señor Rivera by Señorita Medina and Miss Sanderson. Would it not be better to hear the information directly from the participants?"

On the opposite side of the conference table, Avila sat with his fingers laced across his large stomach. He pulled his chin back into the fatty folds of his throat as he considered the interruption. "This is not a court of law, Señor Aguilar, it is a hearing to decide if we will press charges against these women." He pointed at Yasmin and Jessica, then continued speaking to Luis. "You do not need to address me as Your Honor, and your rules of hearsay do not apply. Our employee is merely recounting the information as he knows it."

Luis politely dipped his head, "Yes, of course." He said, his tone betraying just the smallest bit of frustration.

When Rivera had finished speaking, Luis Aguilar politely raised his hand signaling he would like to speak. "Señor Avila, with your indulgence we would like to explain a bit of the family background." He indicated Señora Medina, "This lady is the grandmother of Señorita Yasmin Medina. She has information that your committee might find enlightening."

César Avila nodded his head, "Very well. You may speak next, Señora Medina."

Maria fanned herself gently as she peered from under her lowered eyelashes. "I fear this whole problem is my fault," she said softly. "I have many times recounted the legend of our family being descendants of *La Trigueña* to my granddaughter Yasmin. It was a fascinating bedtime-tale for a small child. She begged me to tell her the same story, over and over again."

Luis politely rolled his hand, prompting her to continue her story.

Sighing emotionally, Maria placed her folded fan on her lap. "Even though I am convinced that this treasure rightfully belongs to our family, we would have advised the authorities of our discovery as soon as we knew the exact location." She gently fanned herself again, demurely looking towards but not directly at the committee kingpin. "It was never anyone's intention to steal this valuable treasure from the citizens of Mexico." She placed her fan on her lap, using her expressive eyes to beseech the chairman for leniency. "Señor, what can we do to fix this problem?"

"Well," sputtered the president of the committee, "first of all, your granddaughter and her friend must turn over any items belonging to the people of Mexico, immediately."

"Yes, of course." Maria turned to look at her granddaughter, smiling supportively.

Before speaking, Yasmin glanced down. Her grandmother's right hand was partially concealed under her fan, fingers crossed in a superstitious wish for good luck. Yasmin opened her purse and carefully pulled out several objects. She gently unwrapped the metal flask that they had taken from the Pirate Mundaca's tomb, and keeping her gaze fixed on the object she recounted the fabricated story that Jessica and she had agreed upon.

"This is the flask that we found mixed in with my grandmother's old family keepsakes. Rolled inside we found a letter written by Mundaca to La Trigueña." Yasmin held up the plastic page protector by one edge and handed the letter to the chairman. "It has a map, of sorts, on the back."

Unwrapping the coins, Yasmin continued addressing the chairman. "As for treasure, we only have these three coins." She gently slid the coins to the middle of the table towards the chairman. "Kirk Patterson stole the others, just as the tropical storm struck."

"Yes, I see," intoned the chairman, "Anything else?"

She trembled slightly as she tilted her chin up, indicating the scabbed-over knife wound. "Just this souvenir that Kirk Patterson gave me when he grabbed the coins."

A buzz of excited words erupted from the committee members. "Oh my God," exclaimed the chairman. "We had no idea that he had threatened your life, Señorita Medina." Turning to Jorge Rivera, he demanded, "Where is this villain now?"

"We have no idea. He escaped during the worst part of the storm." Nodding his head towards Javier Cordillo, he said, "My investigator couldn't locate any sign of him in the park. The rain had obliterated his tracks." Jorge shrugged slightly. "We really have no idea if he is still on the island, or even in Mexico. We have checked with passport control and the airports. Nothing. He could have easily hired a private boat to take him back to the USA."

Flicking her attention from Rivera back to the INAH group on the other side of the table, Yasmin watched as they bent their heads towards the *boss-man, the jefe,* quietly conferring amongst themselves. The chairman of the group finally nodded in agreement, and the committee members leaned back in their chairs.

César Avila shifted his gaze to Yasmin and Jessica. "It is the finding of this committee that we will not pursue the charges of illegal treasure hunting on national property." He solemnly dipped his head politely to Maria Medina. "Your gracious grandmother has explained everything. You may keep the antique flask and the map as they were part of Señora Medina's personal collection; however, the coins belong to the people of Mexico," he added, moving the three gold coins closer. "You must stay away from the park until our excavation team has thoroughly searched the area for the remaining treasure. Do you understand?" He pointed a finger sternly at the younger women.

Relieved, and speechless with gratitude, they both eagerly nodded their heads, eventually finding the words to answer the chairman. "Of course, yes we do. Thank you so, so much." Reaching to her left, Yasmin tightly squeezed her grandmother's hand, whispering, "Thank you, thank you, thank you."

Maria Medina squeezed back but remained silent, indicating with a slight tilt of her head that they should speak later, in private.

Once again Carlos hungered to hold Yasmin, to congratulate her, to tell her he had been desperately worried. But here they were in a crowd of people standing on a public street, with no chance to speak privately. Frustrated, he turned and grasped Luis' hand, pulling him into a bear hug. "Gracias amigo, thank you so much for helping." He quietly added, "Give me the bill, and I will bring the money to you today."

Luis grinned, "No worries. We'll work something out." He flapped his hand dismissively. "Besides, that was fun. Something different from the same old lawyer stuff. It's not every day a guy gets to help two beautiful women out of trouble." Then glancing at Maria Medina, he added "Excuse me, Señora Medina, I meant three beautiful women."

Maria Medina smiled warmly and leaned towards the younger man, giving him a quick kiss on the cheek. "Thank you so much for helping my granddaughter and Jessica." She shook her head and sighed, "Now I have to explain to her *papi*, my son, what his beloved daughter has been up to for the past few weeks."

Yasmin interjected, "No abuela, it is my problem. I will tell *papi*."

Her grandmother raised her eyebrows, "Ayieee. That will be an interesting conversation."

Carlos surreptitiously checked the time on his Rolex. He was expecting a text from Diego or Pedro. Hopefully there hadn't been any problems. What he needed was a small distraction until he heard from the guys that everything had gone according to plan. Carlos clapped his hands together and said, "Well, I think this calls for a small celebration at the *Loco Lobo*. Lunch is on me."

Chapter 40

November 15th Late afternoon

Diego Avalos bent over the trussed-up figure of Kirk Patterson; his lips pulled back in a snarling smile. "Well amigo, your little adventure is almost over. This is where we say adios."

In a sudden burst of energy, Patterson struggled frantically against his bonds, kicking at Diego, curses smothered by the tightly wrapped duct tape sealing his mouth. He jerked side to side, bending and flopping on the deck, trying to pull free.

"Nice try, *pendejo*. You are wrapped up tighter than a Christmas turkey and not going anywhere." Diego smiled a toothy crocodile-grin. "I've been tying strong knots since I was a little *niño* helping my *papi* on his fishing *panga*. If I made a mistake, *papi* would give me a slap on the head, and he had big, hard hands, so I only made a mistake once." Pointing his chin, he signalled that Pedro should grab Kirk's feet. Patterson was too long and awkward for him to lift alone.

"Okay, let's do this," Pedro said, as they lifted the bundled form to the height of the railings. "Ready? On three." The boat rocked slightly underfoot as the two big men swung Kirk in time to the count, "One. Two. Three," and released him on the word three. They watched impassively as Patterson sailed through the air and landed on a wooden wharf with a meaty thump, emitting a muffled scream as his body tumbled along the rough surface.

"Sorry about the wood splinters in your ass," Diego chuckled as he tossed him a mock wave, "maybe a nice three-hundred-pound jailbird will help you remove the slivers."

Pedro released the bow line and motioned that Diego should get the stern line. "Send the text, and let's get the hell out of here." He pulled one of twin throttles into reverse and set the other in forward, expertly turning the big cruiser one-hundred-and-eighty degrees as they cleared the dock. "We need fuel. I know a friendly marina that won't ask questions," Pedro said as he spun the wheel and goosed the engines.

Diego nodded that he had heard while he thumbed his phone contact list. Finding Carlos' number, he sent a one-word text: *Finito*. He sighed tiredly, hoping that their return trip would be uneventful, without any visits from a suspicious

Coast Guard cutter. It would be pretty hard to explain what two Mexicans were doing in Florida, driving a fast sport-fishing boat. Delivering a package for a friend just wasn't going to cut it as an explanation.

At the *Loco Lobo,* Carlos smiled with relief when he finally received the text from Diego. He excused himself from the celebrating group, ducked into his office, and firmly closed the door. He quickly scrolled through his recent calls, looking for the number of his American friend, a Florida cop who had retired to a cottage on the beach in the Florida Keys. The call was answered on the second ring.

"Hey there, bud. How're you doing?" the American drawled in Carlos' ear.

"I'm good," Carlos replied, tensely skipping past the traditional polite conversation questions of "how are you and your family?" "That package that I mentioned has been delivered. Can you arrange an immediate pickup?"

"Already on it. I noticed a sleek looking vessel entering my cove a few minutes ago. We arrived at the dock just as they were headed out. We already have the parcel." He chuckled, "It's a bit banged up, but otherwise okay."

Carlos replied, "I want a delivery, not a disposal."

The older man nodded for emphasis even though Carlos couldn't see him. "Yeah, no worries," he replied. It's easier to hand him over to the Sheriff's Department than to find an alligator willing to eat this mangy dog."

"Okay, thanks again Alfie." Carlos said, "Anytime I can return the favor, please call."

"Sure. Pleasure doing business with you. Adios amigo."

Alfie turned to grin at a younger man standing beside a dark blue Ford 4 x 4 truck. The man was well-built, wearing a baseball cap pulled low over his eyes that were hidden behind dark sunglasses.

Adjusting his own ball cap and wraparound sunglasses, Alfie stared down at Kirk, laying in the bed of the pickup. He nudged Patterson's arm with the end of an aluminum baseball bat. Back in the day when he was still a young beat cop, it had been his backup weapon for rowdy prisoners. *Couldn't get away with that nowadays*, he mused.

"So, Mr. Patterson, or should I say, Mr. Johnson, how do you like our Florida hospitality so far?" he said, nudging Kirk a bit harder with the end of the bat, causing him to thrash around like a fish hooked on a line. "Now, son, you just relax. Just a short ride and you'll be all comfy cozy in our local jail."

He smirked, then reached over and secured Patterson's trussed up form with rope to the cargo hooks on either side of the pickup box. "You'll forgive me if I don't introduce myself and my young friend here, but we'd like to remain as incognito as possible." He pulled at the ropes, testing his knots and nodding to himself that he had done a good job, as he continued to taunt Kirk. "That's just in case a fine upstanding citizen like yourself decides to pay us a visit at a future date, assuming of course that you don't get a death sentence from our delightful Florida justice system." Then he dropped a tarp over Kirk. "Have a nice nap, son."

"Okay, make the call to your boss," he said to his collaborator. "Sheriff Johnson will be pleased as punch to have the publicity from catching a murderer this close to his re-election."

Chapter 41

December 30th Afternoon

Carlos leaned back in his office chair, his interlocked hands cradling his head while he stretched his tired back muscles. *Wow. These last few weeks have been crazy.*

TV Isla Mujeres was the first to broadcast the story of Jessica and Yasmin finding the pirate Captain Lorencillo de Graaf's treasure. Hard to believe that gold demanded as ransom for the release of the Mayor of Veracruz in 1683 ended up on Isla Mujeres, to be rediscovered two hundred years later by Fermin Mundaca, and then again by Yasmin and Jessica. It was a great story filled with murder and mayhem, kidnapping and ransom. The public loved it.

Once the story broke, dozens of reporters for state and national news outlets had descended on the island, filming the excavation and the treasure. INAH had dug up some very interesting artifacts.

There were two ancient Spanish swords, a few gemstones, and one gold goblet that was absolutely beautiful. The goblet was probably looted by the pirates from the cathedral in Veracruz. Not all seventy-thousand pieces of eight had been located, but it was possible that Mundaca had used some of the treasure for living expenses between the time he discovered it and the time he died. Or, as Jessica had pointed out, according to the pirate articles of agreement, the captain would have only kept two or possibly three shares of the ransom for himself, dividing the rest amongst the crew.

Even though Yasmin and Jessica's actions had been a bit iffy, the news outlets were hailing them as heroines for locating the treasure. There was even a mention of Jessica's mutt, Sparky, sniffing out the gold. That in itself was an amazing story.

The winter festivities in Mexico had come and gone in a flurry of celebrations starting December 16th with the *posadas*, then *Noche Buena*, and finally Christmas Day. In two more days they would be celebrating New Year's Eve. It was hard to believe the year was almost over.

Carlos straightened up, deciding to do a quick check on the lunchtime crowd at the *Loco Lobo*. Business was brisk as the visiting news and camera crews wanted interviews and photos of Jessica and

Yasmin at work. Good for his business, but slightly annoying for the two women.

He sauntered out to the restaurant, greeting regular customers by name and stopping to chat with visitors. Glancing over at a corner table, he noticed Pedro and Diego sitting in their regular spot. Diego's legs, too long to fit comfortably under the small restaurant table, were taking up space in the aisle. A tripping hazard for sure, but the staff were accustomed to dodging his lengthy femurs. With the addition of the fresh but rapidly dying Christmas tree in the corner, complete with the traditional holiday decorations, the guys looked a bit crowded in their usual spot. The tree would remain up until after the *Día de los Reyes* (Kings Day) on January 6th, the traditional gift-giving night for families, more important than Christmas in the Latino culture.

"Hey guys, good to see you. Got everything you need?" Carlos asked, as he did their usual macho-guy fist bump and hand slap greeting. He had been very relieved when his two friends had safely returned to the island after delivering Kirk Patterson to the State Police in Florida. The thirty-hour round trip wasn't the problem; it was the potential for running into American authorities who would have taken a dim view of the whole kidnapping-illegal entry thing, even though they were returning a criminal to the Florida police.

Diego held up a half-empty pint glass of an amber-colored liquid, "What the hell is this stuff? Jessica recommended it."

Carlos smiled, "Pale Ale, a hand-crafted microbrew, made on the island by Isla Brewing Company."

"Huh, well whatever it is, it tastes good." Diego tipped up the glass, draining the contents, then placed the empty glass on the tabletop. "I wouldn't say no to another one." He quirked an eyebrow at Carlos.

Carlos turned his head, smiling as he glanced at Yasmin. He did a finger twirl over the table and pointed at himself, meaning another round for this table and put it on my tab.

Yasmin beamed back in acknowledgement, adding a Diet Coke to the order for Carlos. As she organized the drinks, she contemplated their recent adventure. Thankfully, things were starting to normalize again. With all the publicity in the news and Facebook chatter, she and Jessica were considered minor celebrities on the island. It was exciting at first; now it was becoming a huge pain.

Her grandmother, the formidable Maria Medina, had insisted that she be the one to break the news to Yasmin's family before it became public knowledge. Maria had softened her son's irritation at Yasmin's uncharacteristically illicit behavior. In the end he had seen the humorous side of the events and was very thankful that his daughter was not going to prison. In the years to come it would be a story retold many times at family reunions.

On the other hand, Jessica's parents and siblings had been intrigued to hear about their treasure hunting adventure. Yasmin had sat supportively beside Jessica as she recounted the story using the video phone app, Facetime, carefully editing out a few of the scandalous details like the risk of imprisonment and being threatened by a knife-wielding psychopath. No sense in worrying everyone needlessly. Since Kirk Patterson's sudden disappearance, the local news outlets merely referred to him as an unknown thief.

Even Ryan Whitecross had been cleared of wrongdoings by INAH. He had stopped by a few days ago to apologize for tagging along with Kirk. Despite his sincere and lengthy apology, he was not someone that Yasmin wanted to be friends with. Thankfully, he had returned to Minneapolis and his job after repeatedly apologizing to both her and Jessica.

Yasmin signaled Jessica that she had a drink order for Carlos. Jessica shook her head, pointing at a big table where she was in the middle of taking orders. Yasmin nodded, then turned to Isabella, her assistant. "Can you handle the bar for a few minutes? I'll just take this order over to Carlos and the guys."

"Sure." Isabella agreed, winking. "Good luck, chica."

Yasmin's mouth twitched a little. Lifting the tray of drinks, she ambled in her long-legged easy stride towards their table. Okay, maybe she was being a bit obvious, but she just wanted Carlos to loosen up a little and stop being afraid of her. She was pretty sure he was interested, but he was as tense as a teenage boy on his first date every time she was near. Maybe it was up to her to make the first move.

Her heart beat a little faster as she imagined running her fingers through Carlos' short dark hair. She loved his hair, his awesome butt, and his generous heart. Standing beside Carlos, she felt him stiffen as her elbow brushed his arm as she reached to place the drinks on the table. "What are all of you handsome men doing for New Year's Eve?" she asked, mentally rolling her eyes at how absolutely juvenile that question had sounded.

Ever the group clown, Diego dramatically placed his crossed hands over his heart, staring soulfully into her eyes. "Yasmin, Yasmin, my one true love. I do not wish to break your heart, but my wife and I will be celebrating in Centro along with our four children." His mouth quirked into a sly grin. "Perhaps you could babysit our youngest, while my Cristina and I dance until dawn?"

She laughed at his silliness, realizing that Diego had probably picked up on the increased tension between herself and Carlos, and was trying to loosen things up a bit.

Changing tactics, Diego grinned and pointed at the newspaper he had been reading. "Hey, did you see this article about our friend Kirk Patterson?" he asked, showing Yasmin the title of the lead article *Murderer on Trial in Florida*.

Yasmin picked the publication off the table, quickly scanning the article. Patterson was only being tried on the rape charges, but murder charges for two young women were still being considered. A lack of hard evidence connecting Patterson to the women was hampering the Florida prosecutor. Fingers crossed he wouldn't return to Isla Mujeres, ever again. Both Jessica and Yasmin had been sleeping better knowing he was in prison.

Strangely enough there was absolutely no mention of the Spanish coins being in his possession when he was arrested. The island coconut telegraph was in full force, speculating on where he had stashed the gold before his arrest. Or maybe a Florida cop was considerably richer. Mexican policía frequently demanded bribes for small traffic violations and such, so in local opinion it stood to reason that the arresting cops had probably kept the gold.

She handed the newspaper back to Diego and stretched out her hand to pick up her tray just as Carlos reached to hand it to her. Their fingers touched, and he lightly applied pressure while smiling into her eyes. She could feel her insides turn to liquid contained in a covering of hot skin. She wanted nothing more than to grab him tightly and hold on for the ride.

Oh. My. What a ride that would be.

Chapter 42

December 31st Early morning

Tossing aside the light blanket and sheet, Jessica hopped out of bed and checked the time on her phone. Yep, lots of time to enjoy her usual two cups of strong dark brew and then take Sparky for a long walk before getting ready for work. December 31st—it was a perfect day to start her exercise regime for the new year. Get up early. Spend an hour walking. Eat better, and drink only wine, beer and lots of water. No more nasty margaritas. Well, okay, no more nasty margaritas for a month, more or less, or as Yasmin liked to say, *más o menos*.

Tomorrow, New Year's Day, would be a bit iffy on the exercise front because she and Yasmin had reserved a table in the square for the all-night celebrations. They were expecting hordes of friends to stop by and toast the dawn with a glass of bubbly, or as Yasmin called it, 'giggle juice', because *Prosecco* made her giggly. By walking today, she could avoid feeling guilty tomorrow.

"Good morning, Sparky," she chirped, feeling extremely righteous about her new plan. "Let's call Yasmin. I'm sure she would absolutely love to be awake at eight in the morning." Multi-tasking, she opened the door for Sparky as she poked the keys for Yasmin's number. "Pees and poops. Pees and poops."

"Peas and what?" Yasmin asked, not quite sure why someone was reciting names of vegetables to her. "Jessica, is that you?" Propped up on one elbow in bed, she stretched and yawned, then looked at the time. *Eight o'clock. Was that woman nuts?*

"Rise and shine. We're going walking. I'm going to take better care of myself this year." Jessica poured her first cup of coffee, adding a tiny bit of non-fat milk, just enough, according to her dentist, to avoid caffeine stains on her teeth. "If you hurry up, you can have a cup of my dee-licious coffee as your reward."

"Uff. Okay, give me twenty minutes. You'd better have that cup of coffee ready for me."

Forty minutes later the two women and Sparky arrived at the entrance to the Hacienda Mundaca Park. Yasmin had argued against returning to the park, convinced that the authorities would be waiting to pounce.

"Oh, for heaven's sake," countered Jessica, "we are just going for a walk in the park. I'm curious. I want to see how big and how deep the excavation was for the treasure."

"Fine. But if we get tossed in jail, I'm going to blame it all on you. I am just the innocent bystander, the naïve local girl led astray by the *gringa loca* — again." As Yasmin sauntered towards the park gates, she noticed the same woman at the entrance. "Buenos Dias Adela," she cheerily called, handing over the admission fee and extending her wrist for the application of the paper wrist band.

Adela Yam grinned. "Ah, the two famous treasure hunters have returned. What will you be digging up this time?" She bent and patted Sparky's head. "And I see you have brought your equally famous gold-sniffing dog. Remember, the *cocodrilo* enjoys the taste of dogs, famous or not-famous, it doesn't matter to him." Her toothy smile indicated she was teasing.

Familiar with Adela's dark humor, Jessica returned the smile, "Sparky's not afraid of that smelly old crocodile," she bent and patted the dog, "are you little man?"

Light laughter followed the two women as they wandered along the gravel pathway, heading in the general direction of the excavation site. Jessica ambled slowly along behind Sparky, who as usual was intently investigating the pathway and surrounding vegetation. About every two or three strides he would stop, lift his back leg and add his own brand of scent to a plant or rock. *He was a bottomless fountain of liquid*, mused Jessica.

December to May was the dry winter season in Mexico, and the ground in the park was baked hard. The tangled growth was brown, a mass of thin branches and a few leaves. Neglected and spindly, the deep pink bougainvillea continued to flower, adding color to the gray stone benches, crumbling remnants of Fermin Mundaca's garden of love, the garden he created for a woman almost forty years younger than himself, a woman who rejected his unwelcome attention.

Deeper in the park, the entrance to the collapsed cave was fenced by a rudimentary wooden structure, not substantial enough to block access. Only the fear of reprisal from the federal government would keep people from entering. Jessica lightly placed her forearms on the top wooden rail, leaning forward for a better view. "Wow. Big hole. Sparky would have had to dig a long way to find all of the treasure."

Yasmin stared longingly at the excavation. "So close, and yet so far. I wonder what happened to the coins and things that Kirk Patterson took from us back in November."

"Yeah, it kind of pisses me off." Jessica said with an acidic bite in her voice. "We do all the work, and he gets rich."

"Not exactly rich. He is in a Florida jail awaiting trial for rape and maybe murder. Thank goodness for that." Yasmin shivered at the memory of her recent encounter with Kirk, or Kyle, whatever his real name was. The scar under her chin from his knife cut had faded from bright red to a thinner pink line. Her doctor said the scar would slowly fade over time, but she knew it wasn't likely to ever fade from her memory.

"Well, just a big hole in the ground and not much else." Jessica straightened up and tugged lightly on Sparky's leash. "Time to head back."

"Let's take the other pathway past Mundaca's house. It's a quicker route back to the park gates." Yasmin pointed to her left.

The little group slowly progressed downhill towards Mundaca's modest dwelling, in time to Sparky's marking preferences. Stop, squirt, walk. Stop, squirt, walk. Or at least he went through the motions of scent marking, having finally depleted his internal reservoir.

As they neared the pirate's house, Jessica felt a sudden forceful yank on the dog's leash. "What?" she muttered, as the nylon lead slipped through her fingers. "Sparky, stop! Stop!" Running after the escaping mutt, she cussed. "Damn it all to hell, dog. What is the matter with you?"

"Jessica, be careful. Maybe he smells the crocodile!" Yasmin warned.

"Sparky! Sparky, stop!"

With his butt in the air and his tail wagging furiously, Sparky tugged relentlessly on something that was underneath the thick bushes.

"What are you doing?" demanded Jessica when she caught up to her dog.

A wide sloppy grin on his face, Sparky dropped a heavy mud-caked bag at her feet. Her bag. The one Kirk had snatched from them during the storm.

El Fin

And there are more Isla Mujeres Mysteries!

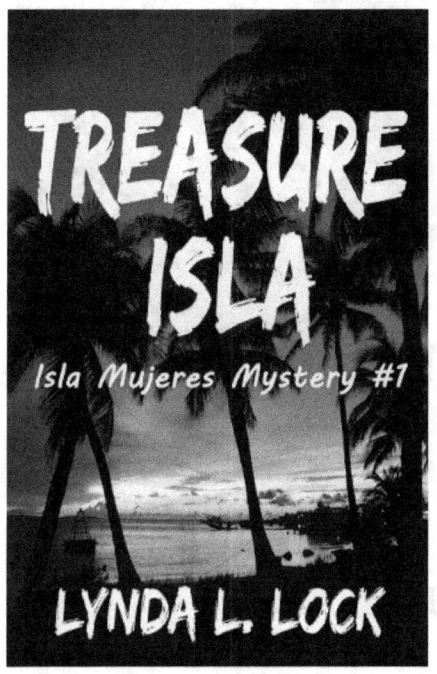

Treasure Isla Book #1

Treasure Isla is a humorous Caribbean adventure set on Isla Mujeres, a tiny island off the eastern coast of Mexico. Two twenty-something women find themselves in possession of a seemingly authentic treasure map, which leads them on a chaotic search for buried treasure while navigating the dangers of too much tequila, disreputable men, and a killer. And there is a dog, a lovable rescue mutt.

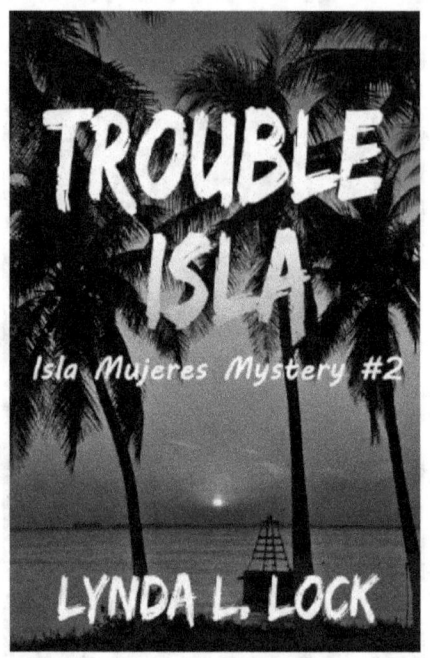

Trouble Isla Book #2

"This pair of leading ladies are fun to immerse in for an afternoon escape. The character development is richly layered and entertaining. The stakes are also enjoyably high, and the action sequences will keep readers voraciously flipping pages. Trouble Isla is a quick, unpredictable read. Bringing this small Caribbean island to life, and populating it with vivid characters that will continue to carry this series forward, Lynda L. Lock has created a uniquely colorful mystery." Self-Publishing Review, ★★★★

Tormenta Isla Book #3

A mysterious disappearance of a local man and the looming threat of multiple hurricanes headed toward the peaceful Caribbean island of Isla Mujeres creates havoc in the lives of Jessica, her friends and her rescue mutt, Sparky. - Diego held up his smartphone and silently showed her the screen, pointing at the NOAA graphics.

Her eyes opened wide in surprise as she looked at the screen, then a frown crinkled her brow. "Really? Three hurricanes?"

"*Si*," he responded, "Pablo, Rebekah, y Sebastien."

Temptation Isla Book #4

Rafael Fernandez leaned forward resting his elbows on the polished wood, tapping his finger-tips together. "Take them all out! At the reception." He said, sweeping his right hand in a side-ways motion as if he was knocking a pile of papers from his desk to the floor.

"As you wish, Don Rafael." Alfonso Fuentes' jaw muscle twitched with tension.

"You don't agree?" Fernandez snarled.

Alfonso paused momentarily considering his next words. He had to get this exactly right or he would, at the very least, be demoted to the riskiest tasks or in the worse-case scenario killed for insubordination.

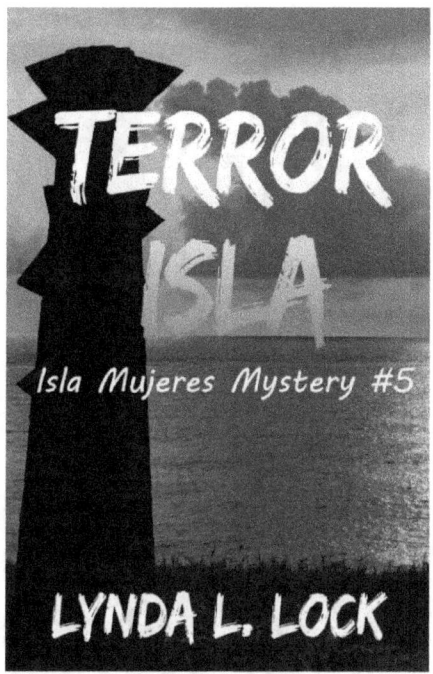

Terror Isla Book #5

Isla Mujeres, a tiny island paradise in the Caribbean Sea, is rocked by a power struggle between a Mexican cartel and a Romanian gang as they battle for control of the illegitimate ATM skimming. Big changes are coming for Carlos and Yasmin, while Jessica Sanderson fends off an angry lover from her past. Sparky, Jessica's stocky beach mutt is once again at the center of another Sparky-situation.

"I want a super-hero cape. A red one," Diego Avalos said. "I am feeling very underappreciated."

"In Jessica's opinion, Sparky is the super-hero with the red cape. We're just his minions doing his bidding," Pedro rejoined. "I'll pick you up in ten minutes."

Twisted Isla Book #6

Death stalks the annual Island Time Music Festival. Nashville musicians and songwriters flock to the tropical island of Isla Mujeres to raise funds for the Little Yellow School House. Jessica and her keen-nosed beach-mutt Sparky are thrown into another murder mystery.

Sergeant Ramirez held up his palm with his fingers spread wide, "That's the fifth."

"Fifth what?" Asked Mike Lyons."

"Body," answered Ramirez, his eyes sweeping to Jessica's face, "that we've had to question señorita Sanderson about."

"Really?" Mike lobbed a startled look at Jessica.

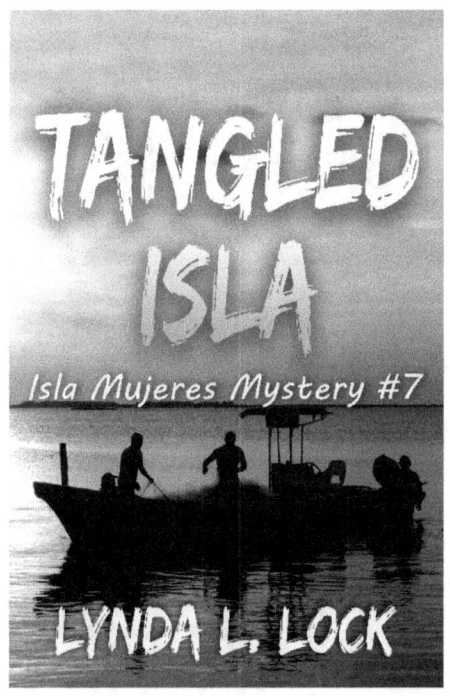

Tangled Isla Book #7

Leading up to the busiest time of the year on Isla Mujeres, four young women similar in appearance to the Florida victims, are unaccounted for and have been reported as missing by concerned friends.

Longing for a reunion with her island friends, Jessica Sanderson returns to Mexico on a solo visit, leaving her partner Mike Lyons with the challenging task of babysitting her legendary and finicky dog, Sparky.

When Jessica arrives on the island she is persuaded to participate in the annual children's parade, wearing the Minnie Mouse costume. The parade is disrupted by an unexplained event, and Jessica becomes entangled in the mystery of the missing women.

CORKED #1 Death in the Vineyards

Love, lust, and loot in the affluent world of wine and wineries.

CORKED, is the newest murder mystery from the author of the exciting Isla Mujeres Mysteries. Murder follows Jessica Sanderson and her detective dog Sparky as they relocate from their Caribbean paradise in Mexico to the Okanagan wine country in Canada. On Isla Mujeres, big changes are coming for Jessica's friends as the COVID19 virus gains momentum. Leaving her beloved island Jessica follows her new love interest, Mike Lyons, into a new adventure.

SMASHED #2 Death in the Vineyards

Some people can convince themselves they can do no wrong.

While wildfires ravage the Okanagan Valley, Jessica Sanderson and her love interest Mike Lyons battle to save two wineries; one from the massive wildfire that is threatening homes and businesses in Okanagan Falls, and the other from economic disaster and the sudden death of their winemaker.

In *SMASHED*, Jessica and her Mexi-mutt Sparky find themselves in the middle of a sticky situation. In this highly-anticipated sequel to *CORKED*, inquisitive Jessica and the amazing nose of Sparky are once again caught up in a police investigation.

CRUSHED #3 Death in the Vineyards

Sometimes tragedy strikes from a clear blue sky.

While creating a new life for themselves in the Okanagan Valley's wine region, Jessica Sanderson and Mike Lyons become entangled in another unexpected death.

CRUSHED takes us a wild ride of intertwined tragedies, family secrets, and substance abuse, while RCMP Corporal Caitlin Smith races to solve the murder and unravel the surrounding mystery. Will Jessica's Mexican beach mutt, Sparky, and his keen nose again help with the investigation?

Grab your copy today, and join the adventure.

Hola amigos y amigas

Pardon my lack of Spanish. I keep trying to learn, but every night while I am sleeping the words leak out of my brain and onto the pillow.

In a perfect world, I would have written this story in Spanish or in this case Isla-Spanish which is a colorful mix of local expressions and a bit of Mayan tossed in for added flavor.

However, most of my readers are English speaking. So, for the purpose of this story, the local folks are fluent in both Spanish and English, especially the cuss words.

I chose to *italicize* only a few of the less familiar Spanish expressions.

Like every self-published writer, I rely heavily on recommendations and reviews to sell my books. If you enjoyed reading any of my *Isla Mujeres Mysteries* or my *Death in the Vineyards* novels please leave a review on Amazon, Goodreads, Bookbub, Facebook or Twitter. Tell your friends, tell your family, or anyone who will listen. Word of mouth is enormously helpful.

If you come across an annoying blunder, please contact me via one of my social media accounts and I will make it disappear.

Facebook @ Lynda L Lock
Instagram @ Lynda Lock
Amazon @ Lynda L Lock
Bookbub @ Lynda L Lock
Goodreads @ Lynda L Lock
A Writer's Life blog

Bilingual books for children

Acknowledgements

Writing is a solitary obsession, with hours spent creating, correcting, and considering the words on the computer screen. However, I have had assistance from some amazing people:

First and foremost, I would like to acknowledge Fidel Villanueva Madrid, our respected island historian for his fascinating stories and comprehensive research.

Ronda Winn Roberts, for her very informative article on pirates.

Tony Garcia, for the beautiful cover photos for three of the *Isla Mujeres Mysteries*, plus the photo of Sparky and me.

Carmen Amato, mystery writer and creator of the Emilia Cruz Detective Series, who designed the cover for this book and the sequels.

Freddy Medina, Eva Velázquez, Javier Martinez, Marla Bainbridge, and Patricio Yam Dzul are cherished friends who are always willing to share their stories.

Apache (Isauro Martinez Jr.) is another one of my go-to-friends when I am searching for specific information about the island.

Manuscript and proofreaders include Lawrie Lock, Richard Grierson, Linda Grierson, Betsy Garcia Snider, Déanne Gray, Rob Goth, Julie Andrews Goth, Shirley Andrews, Sue McDonald Lo, Janice Carlisle Rodgers, and Kim Lawton.

My great-niece, Ellen Fallis, for helping me update my lingo.

And a very special thanks to Editor Michael Rowley, for helping me pull this story together. Any and all remaining mistakes are mine.

Thank you, thank you, and thank you all!

About the author

Born in a British Columbia, Canada, gold mining community that is now essentially a ghost town, Lynda has had a diverse, and some might say eccentric, working career. Her job history includes bank clerk, antique store owner, ambulance attendant, volunteer firefighter, SkyTrain transit control center supervisor, a partner in a bed and breakfast, a partner in a microbrewery, and hotel manager. The adventure and the experience were always more important than the paycheck.

Writing has always been in the background of her life, starting with travel articles for a local newspaper, an unpublished novel written before her fortieth birthday, and articles for a Canadian safety magazine.

When she and her husband, Lawrie Lock, retired to Isla Mujeres, Mexico, in 2008, they started a weekly blog, Notes from Paradise, to update friends and family on their newest adventure.

Needing something more to keep her active mind occupied, Lynda and island friend Diego Medina self-published two bilingual books for children, *The Adventures of Thomas the Cat / Las Aventuras de Tómas el Gato plus The Adventures of Thomas and Sparky / Las Aventuras de Tómas y Sparky.*

One thing led to another, and Lynda created and self-published the Isla Mujeres Mystery series, set on the island in the Caribbean Sea where they lived. Following the death of Lawrie in 2018, she and Sparky remained in Mexico until the COVID-19 pandemic became a reality.

In March 2020, Lynda and Sparky decided to return to the Okanagan Valley, Canada. Her new series, Death in the Vineyard, combines two things dear to her heart: Canada and good wine.

The legal stuff

Most of the characters and events in this book are fictional; the exception being the famous pirates that are mentioned in the story including Laurens de Graaf, Fermin Mundaca, Nikolaas Van Hoorn, Michel de Grammont, and Pierre Bot.

Island resident Tony Garcia, exceptional photographer and tour boat operator, is well-known local personality who kindly allowed me to use his name in the story.

The Instituto Nacional de Antropología e Historia – the National Institute of Anthropology and History (INAH) does exist, and they do an amazing job of protecting Mexican historical sites. The closest office is located in Cancún. I created the Isla Mujeres branch office.

Isla Brewing Company – Cerveza Isla makes delicious, handcrafted ales that are available in a few select restaurants.

Jessica Sanderson is a product of my imagination but like me, was born in BC Canada and she enjoys critters of any type including mammals, reptiles, amphibians, or insects.

Carlos Mendoza is also purely a product of my imagination. He shares a few characteristics with my husband Lawrie; a good sense of humor, the love of dancing, and a faint facial scar, plus the appreciation of Rolex watches and expensive cars. Lawrie's scar was the result of a horrific car accident at age seventeen.

Yasmin Medina is completely fictitious, but she is tall with curly hair like my friend Yazmin Aguirre. She unfortunately passed away in 2020.

The *Loco Lobo Restaurant* is completely fictitious, it is not based on any location or restaurant.

Any other resemblance to persons, whether living or dead, is strictly coincidental.

Treasure Isla

Published by Lynda L. Lock

Copyright 2016

All rights reserved.

E-book: ISBN 978-0-9936203-1-7

Paperback: ISBN 978-0-9936203-3-1

Hardcover: ISBN 978-1-738-9616-4-1

Spanish expressions

Bruja del Mar – Literally witch of the sea, Sea Witch
Carina – urban slang for a funny, gorgeous girlfriend
Casita – small house
Casa – house
Claro or claro que sí – agreement, of course
Cómo está? – How are you?
Con permiso – to move around or past a person
Cuchi-cuchi – humorous euphemism for sex
Don or Doña – respectful title used with the first name
Hermano – brother, or any male who is like a brother
Hermana – sister, or any female who is like a sister
Hijo de la chingada – crude curse, son of a bitch
Hola – hi or hello
Hombre – man
La Trigueña – The young woman Mundaca loved
Loco Lobo – Crazy Wolf, also El Loco Lobo
Maldito – darn, damn
Mama – mom   Mami – mommy
Mande? – The person didn't hear you.
Más o menos – more or less
Mi amor – my love
Mierda – swear word, shit
Mordidita – bribe, literally a little bite
Motos – motor scooters, motorbikes
Niña(s) – girl or girls
Niño(s) – boy or boys, can also mean children
Papa – dad   Papi – daddy
Pendejo – swear word
Que pasa – what's happening
Que pasó – what happened
Rapido – rapid, fast
Tia – auntie, or an older female who is like an aunt
Tio – uncle, or an older male who is like an uncle
Topes – speed bumps